Erle Stanley Gardner and The Murder Room

››› This title is part of The Murder Room, our series dedicated to making available out-of-print or hard-to-find titles by classic crime writers.

Crime fiction has always held up a mirror to society. The Victorians were fascinated by sensational murder and the emerging science of detection; now we are obsessed with the forensic detail of violent death. And no other genre has so captivated and enthralled readers.

Vast troves of classic crime writing have for a long time been unavailable to all but the most dedicated frequenters of second-hand bookshops. The advent of digital publishing means that we are now able to bring you the backlists of a huge range of titles by classic and contemporary crime writers, some of which have been out of print for decades.

From the genteel amateur private eyes of the Golden Age and the femmes fatales of pulp fiction, to the morally ambiguous hard-boiled detectives of mid twentieth-century America and their descendants who walk our twenty-first century streets, The Murder Room has it all. **›››**

The Murder Room
Where Criminal Minds Meet

themurderroom.com

Erle Stanley Gardner (1889–1970)

Born in Malden, Massachusetts, Erle Stanley Gardner left school in 1909 and attended Valparaiso University School of Law in Indiana for just one month before he was suspended for focusing more on his hobby of boxing that his academic studies. Soon after, he settled in California, where he taught himself the law and passed the state bar exam in 1911. The practise of law never held much interest for him, however, apart from as it pertained to trial strategy, and in his spare time he began to write for the pulp magazines that gave Dashiell Hammett and Raymond Chandler their start. Not long after the publication of his first novel, *The Case of the Velvet Claws*, featuring Perry Mason, he gave up his legal practice to write full time. He had one daughter, Grace, with his first wife, Natalie, from whom he later separated. In 1968 Gardner married his long-term secretary, Agnes Jean Bethell, whom he professed to be the real 'Della Street', Perry Mason's sole (although unacknowledged) love interest. He was one of the most successful authors of all time and at the time of his death, in Temecula, California in 1970, is said to have had 135 million copies of his books in print in America alone.

Bachelors Get Lonely (1961)
Shills Can't Count Chips (1961)
Try Anything Once (1962)
Fish or Cut Bait (1963)
Up For Grabs (1964)
Cut Thin to Win (1965)
Widows Wear Weeds (1966)
Traps Need Fresh Bait (1967)

Doug Selby D.A. series

The D.A. Calls it Murder (1937)
The D.A. Holds a Candle (1938)
The D.A. Draws a Circle (1939)
The D.A. Goes to Trial (1940)
The D.A. Cooks a Goose (1942)
The D.A. Calls a Turn (1944)

The D.A. Takes a Chance (1946)
The D.A. Breaks an Egg (1949)

Terry Clane series

Murder Up My Sleeve (1937)
The Case of the Backward
  Mule (1946)

Gramp Wiggins series

The Case of the Turning Tide
  (1941)
The Case of the Smoking
  Chimney (1943)

Two Clues (two novellas) (1947)

Double or Quits

Erle Stanley Gardner

An Orion book

Copyright © The Erle Stanley Gardner Trust 1941

This edition published by
The Orion Publishing Group Ltd
Orion House
5 Upper St Martin's Lane
London WC2H 9EA

An Hachette UK company
A CIP catalogue record for this book is available from the British Library

ISBN 978 1 4719 0884 2

www.orionbooks.co.uk

chapter 1

THE BIG FISHING BARGE rolled lazily on the backs of incoming swells. It was still too early for the crowd. Only a few scattered fishing poles were cocked at various angles over the rail. To the east, the sun cleared the tops of California's coast range, beat down on the oily surface of the windless sea, and reflected in a glitter of eye-aching glare.

Bertha Cool, as solid and as competent as a coil of barbed wire, sat in the director's chair, her feet propped on the rail, a long bamboo pole held steadily. Her calm gray eyes, diamond-hard and watchful, were fastened on the line just where it entered the water, watching for that first little jerk.

She reached in the pocket of her sweater, pulled out a cigarette, and fitted it to her mouth without taking her eyes off the fishline. "Got a match?" she asked.

I propped my fish pole against the rail, held it in position with my knees, struck a match, cupped the flame in my hands, and held it across to her cigarette.

"Thanks," she said, sucking in a deep drag of smoke.

Bertha's sickness had dropped her down to a hundred and sixty pounds. As she got her strength back, she began to go fishing. The outdoor life was making her brown and hard. She still tipped the beam at a hundred and sixty, but now it was solid muscle.

The man on my right, a heavy-set individual who gave the impression of wheezing as he breathed, said, "Not much doing, is there?"

"Nope."

"You've been here quite a little while, haven't you?"

"Uh huh."

"You two together?"

1

"Yes."

"Caught anything at all?"

"A few."

We fished for a while in silence, then he said, "I don't care whether I get anything or not. It's so much fun being out where you can relax, inhale the salt air, and get away from the infernal din of civilization."

"Uh huh."

"I get so a telephone bell sounds as ominous as a bomb." He laughed, almost apologetically, and said, "And it seems only yesterday, when I was starting my practice, that I'd keep watching the telephone, as though looking at it would make it ring. Just like your— Pardon me. She isn't your wife or—"

"No."

He said, "I started to call her your mother, and then I realized you never can tell these days. Well, anyway, she's watching the fishline just as I used to watch the telephone, trying to make something happen."

"Lawyer?" I asked him.

"Doctor."

After a little while he said, "That's the way with us doctors. We get so busy safeguarding the health of other people, we neglect our own. It's a constant grind. Operations in the morning, then hospital calls. Office every afternoon. Visits in the evening, and invariably someone who's been nursing a pain all day will wait until you're just getting comfortably settled in bed to call and ask you to come over."

"On a vacation?" I asked him.

"No, just playing hooky—trying to do it every Wednesday." He hesitated, then added, "I have to. Doctor's orders."

I looked at him. He was a little too heavy. The tops of his eyelids were puffed a little so that when he lowered his lids he seemed to have a little trouble getting them back up. His skin was pale. Something about him made me think of a batch of dough which had been put on the back of the stove to raise.

He said, "Your friend certainly looks fit."

"She is. She's my boss."

"Oh."

Bertha might or might not have been listening. She kept her eyes on her fishing line as a cat watches a gopher hole. There was nothing indefinite about Bertha when she wanted something. Right now she wanted fish.

"You say you work for her?"

"Yes."

His forehead showed he was puzzled.

"She runs a detective agency," I explained. "B. Cool—Confidential Investigations. We're taking a day off—in between cases."

"Oh," he said.

Bertha's eyes grew harder. She tensed her muscles, leaned slightly forward, motionless, waiting.

The tip of her pole bent down. Bertha clamped her right hand on the handle of her reel. Her diamonds glittered in the morning sunlight. The tip of her pole went down again and stayed down. The line started cutting through the water in a series of swift, irregular patterns.

"Pull in your line," Bertha said to me. "Give me room."

I started to pull in my line. Something gave a terrific jerk, as though trying to pull the pole out of my hands. My own line began hissing through the water.

"Oh, I say," the doctor said. "That's splendid! I'll get out of the way."

He got up and started walking along the rail, then his own pole bent almost double. I saw his eyelids flutter. His face twisted with excitement.

I tried to hang onto my pole. I heard Bertha's voice over on my left say, "Reel him in. Start pumping."

The three of us were busy. Occasionally down in the

3

green depths of the water, I could get the flash of silver as a fish flung himself against the pull of the line.

Bertha braced herself. Her shoulders heaved against the drag of the pole. A big fish leaped out of the water, and Bertha used the momentum of that leap to keep him coming right on up over the rail.

He hit the deck as though he'd been a sack of wet meal, and then started beating the planks with his tail.

The doctor landed his fish.

Mine got away.

The doctor grinned across at Bertha Cool. "Yours is bigger than mine," he said.

Bertha said, "Uh huh."

"Too bad yours got away," the doctor said to me.

Bertha said, "Donald doesn't care."

The doctor looked at me curiously. I said, "I like the air, the exercise, and the feeling of leisure. When I'm on a case, it's an all-out affair. I like to rest in between times."

"Same with me," the doctor said. Bertha looked him over.

From the hot-dog stand at the center of the boat, savory odors came eddying down wind to our nostrils. The doctor said to Bertha, "How about a hot dog?"

"Not now," she said. "Fish are running." She competently detached her hook, slid the big fish into a sack, put on more bait, threw her line over the side.

I didn't put my pole out again, but stood watching Bertha fishing.

She tied into another one within thirty seconds. The doctor got another strike, and his got away. Bertha landed hers. After that, the doctor landed a good-sized one. Bertha got a small one. Then the run was over.

"How about that hot dog?" the doctor asked.

Bertha nodded.

"You?" he asked me.

"Okay."

4

"I'll get 'em," the doctor said. "We should celebrate. You stay here and fish. Will you keep an eye on my pole?"

I told him I would.

The sun had risen higher over the mountains. The morning mists had dispersed. You could see automobiles moving along the paved road which bordered the ocean.

"Who is he?" Bertha asked, her eyes on her fishline.

"A doctor who's been working too hard and not playing enough. His doctor told him to take it easy. I think he wants something."

"Didn't I hear you telling him who I was?"

"Uh huh. I thought he might be interested."

"That's good," she said. "You never can tell where you'll pick up a piece of business," and then, after a moment, added, "He wants something, all right."

The doctor came back with six hot dogs on toasted buns, plenty of pickles and mustard. He ate his first one with relish. The large fish scales that were stuck to his hands didn't take his appetite.

He said to Bertha, "I never would have picked him for a detective. I thought detectives had to be big, tough individuals."

"You'd be surprised about him," Bertha said, flashing me a glance. "He's chain lightning. Brains count in this business."

I saw the swollen-lidded eyes studying me speculatively, then the lids closed, and after a moment fluttered laboriously back open.

Bertha said, "If something's on your mind, for God's sake go ahead and spill it."

He flashed her a startled look. "What? Why, I didn't—" and then he gave way to real shoulder-shaking laughter. "All right," he said, "you win! I've prided myself on diagnosing patients as they walked across the office. It never occurred to me I'd have someone do the same to me. How did you know?"

5

Bertha said, "You were wide open. Ever since Donald told you who I was, you've been sizing us up. What is it?"

The doctor held his second hot dog in his left hand. He took a card case from his pocket, opened it with something of a flourish, and took out two cards. He gave one to Bertha, and one to me.

I glanced at my card, and pushed it in my pocket. I learned that he was Dr. Hilton Devarest, that his hours were by appointment only, that his residence was in a swanky suburban district, and that his office was in the Medical Mutual Building.

Bertha rubbed her thumb over the engraving, snapped the corner of the pasteboard against her nail to determine the quality of the cardboard. Then she slipped it down in her sweater pocket. She said, "The organization's all here—all that counts. I'm Bertha Cool. He's Donald Lam. Let's hear what's bothering you."

Dr. Devarest said, "My problem is really very simple. I've been the victim of a theft. I'd like to get the stuff back. I'll run over the facts. Adjoining my bedroom is a den which is fixed up with a lot of obsolete stuff I've picked up—old X-ray machines, various electrical equipment, a microscope under a glass shell. It makes a very impressive-looking place."

"You work there?" Bertha asked.

His stomach jiggled with amusement. The slightly puffy lids of his eyes lowered, and after a moment fluttered back. "I do not," he said. "The obsolete equipment is simply a stage setting to impress visitors. When I'm bored by company, I plead some research work which has to be done, excuse myself, and go up to my den. All of my guests have seen that den, and have been properly impressed by it. I can assure you that, to a layman, it is very impressive."

"What do you do when you get up there?" Bertha asked.

"In one corner of the room," he said, "is the most comfortable chair I have been able to buy, and a very satisfactory reading-lamp. I sit there and read detective stories."

Bertha nodded approvingly.

Dr. Devarest went on. "Monday night we had some particularly boring guests. I retired to my study. After the guests went home, my wife came upstairs—"

"How does your wife feel about you ducking out and leaving her to entertain the bores?"

The smile left Dr. Devarest's face. "No one ever bores my wife," he said. "She's interested in people, and she—well, she thinks that I'm working."

"You mean that she doesn't know this study setup is a fake?" Bertha asked.

He hesitated, trying to select just the right words.

"Don't you see?" I said to Bertha. "He fitted it up primarily to fool *her*."

Dr. Devarest stared at me. "What makes you say that?"

I said, "You're too smugly satisfied with it. You chuckle every time you think of it. Anyhow, it doesn't make any difference. Go ahead with the story."

"A very discerning young man," he said to Bertha.

"Told you so," she commented dryly. "What happened Monday?"

"My wife was wearing some jewelry. I have a wall safe in the study."

"Something obsolete like the rest of the stuff?" Bertha asked.

"No," he said. "There's nothing obsolete about that safe. It is the last word."

"What happened?"

"My wife gave me the jewelry she was wearing, and asked me to put it in the safe."

"Does she usually do that?"

"No. She said she felt nervous Monday, as though something was going to happen."

"Did it?"

"Yes. The jewelry was stolen."

"Before you put it in the safe?"

"No. Afterward. I put it in the safe, and went to bed. I had a call yesterday morning about six o'clock. It was a ruptured appendix. I rushed to the hospital and operated. Then I had my morning routine of operations."

"Where does your wife ordinarily keep her jewels?"

"Most of the time in a safety-deposit box at the bank. She telephoned my office about noon and wanted to know if I would drive by and open the safe for her before I went to the office."

"She doesn't have the combination?"

Devarest said positively, "I am the only one who knows how to open that safe."

"What did you do?"

"My office nurse relayed the telephone call to me at the hospital. I said I'd drive by the house sometime before two o'clock. I made it about one. I was in pretty much of a hurry. I hadn't eaten either breakfast or lunch, just had a few cups of black coffee. I ran into the house and dashed upstairs."

"Where was your wife?"

"She was with me when I entered my study."

"You opened the safe?" Bertha asked.

"Yes. The jewels were gone."

"Anything else missing?"

He looked at her with the same expression on his face Bertha had when she'd been watching the fishing line. He said shortly, "No. Just the jewel cases. There wasn't much else in the safe. A couple of books of travelers' checks that I keep for emergencies, and some notes on research work I'm doing in connection with nephritis."

"Exactly where was your wife when you opened the safe?"

"She was standing in the door of the study."

"Perhaps," Bertha said, "you didn't lock the safe when you put the jewels in."

He said, "No. That's out."

"I take it the safe hadn't been tampered with."

"No. Whoever opened it had learned the combination."

"How?"

"That's what I don't know."

Bertha asked, "Could anyone have—"

"We know who did it," he said. "That is, we know who knows who did it."

"Who?"

"A young woman named Starr, Miss Nollie Starr—my wife's secretary."

"What about her?"

Dr. Devarest said, "There are times when you doubt the evidence of your own senses. You rub your eyes and wonder if perhaps you aren't dreaming. I felt the same way when I opened the safe. Naturally, my wife asked a good many questions. Those questions served to clarify my impressions. I distinctly remembered having put the jewels in the safe, and spun the combination."

"What's that got to do with the Starr girl?"

"My wife called Miss Starr, told her to notify the police."

"What happened?"

"When the police didn't show up after an hour, my wife tried to find out what was causing the delay. She rang for Miss Starr. Miss Starr had disappeared. The police hadn't been notified. That gave her an extra hour in which to escape."

"Then what?"

"Then the police came out. They tried to develop latent fingerprints on the safe. They found someone had gone over it carefully with an oiled rag. In Miss Starr's room, concealed in an empty cold cream jar, they found the rag."

"Same one?" I asked.

"They were able to demonstrate that it was the same. A certain distinctive brand of gun oil was on the rag. It was the same oil that was on the safe. The half-used bottle of gun oil also was found in Miss Starr's room. Everything indicated a hasty flight. Miss Starr had not taken anything with her. She'd left her toilet articles, even her toothbrush. She'd simply walked out."

"And the police haven't found her?" Bertha asked.

"Not yet."

"What do you want us to do?"

He turned to look out at the ocean, and said, "Until I met you, I hadn't been aware that I wanted anything done, but—well, if you could get in touch with Miss Starr in advance of the police and tell her that if she'll return the missing articles, I'll be willing to let bygones be bygones. I could pay you a good fee."

"Meaning you won't prosecute?" Bertha asked.

"I won't prosecute," he said, "and I'll give her a cash reward in addition."

"How much?"

"One thousand dollars."

He stood on the swaying deck of the barge, looking out across the ocean, waiting for Bertha to say something. I knew the question that was in Bertha's mind. She waited to ask it until her very silence had caused him to turn back toward her.

"What's in it for us?"

Dr. Devarest took me home with him for dinner. He made no bones about introducing me. I was a private detective he'd hired to "supplement the activities of the police."

His house confirmed the impression I'd formed of him. It had cost money to build it, and it was costing money to keep it up. It was Spanish architecture, white stucco, red tile, verandas with wrought-iron grille work, landscape gardening, servants' quarters, Oriental rugs, bathrooms stuck all over the place, big plate-glass windows, rich, heavy drapes, a large patio, fountains, goldfish, cactus gardens, and atmosphere. There was too much food, and it was too rich, too highly spiced.

Mrs. Devarest had double chins, pop eyes, loved her liquor and food, and made inane remarks. Her first name was Colette.

Two members of her family were living with her. Jim Timley was a bronzed young man who evidently went without his hat in a fruitless attempt to cure a baldness that was creeping up the top of his forehead. His hair was dark. There wasn't any wave in it. He kept it cut short on top, and it looked as though the sun had baked all of the life out of it. But his eyes were a clear, steady hazel. He had a good-looking mouth, and even, regular white teeth which showed when he smiled. The way he gripped my hand indicated he went in for outdoor sports in a big way. He was Mrs. Devarest's nephew, the son of a dead brother.

The other member of her family was a niece of Mrs. Devarest, a Mrs. Nadine Croy who had a little girl named Selma, about three years old. Selma had an early dinner in her nursery and then went to bed. I didn't see her that night. Mrs. Croy was the daughter of Mrs. Devarest's sister. I gathered she had money. She was about twenty-nine, and had quite evidently watched her diet and her figure. She picked her way carefully through the dinner. She had large black eyes that seemed somehow apprehensive. No one said anything about Mr. Croy, so I didn't ask any questions.

There was a wooden-faced butler, and a couple of rather plain women servants. There was a maid named Jeannette who had curves and class. I found out Mrs. Devarest had a chauffeur, but I didn't meet him then. It was his night out. Mrs. Devarest went in for servants and social paraphernalia. Dr. Devarest didn't like to be waited on. He liked to be left alone, whenever he could get away from his practice—which wasn't often.

11

After dinner, Mrs. Devarest handed the doctor a list of calls that had been relayed from his office nurse. He suggested I go up to the study with him while he checked up.

The study was just as he'd described it. I sat down on a chair that was wedged in between a lot of formidable-looking electrical equipment. He settled down in his easy chair, pulled a desk telephone over to him, propped the list of calls up on the chair arm, and said, "Open the door of that electric cardiograph, Lam."

"What's the cardiograph?"

"The one on your right."

I opened the door. There was no wiring in it, but there was a bottle of Scotch, one of bourbon, some glasses, and a siphon of soda.

"Help yourself," he said.

"Some for you?"

"No. I'll have to go out."

I poured myself some Scotch. It was the most expensive brand on the market. Dr. Devarest started twisting the dial on the telephone. He had a nice bedside manner. His voice was very solicitous. Listening to his questions and advice, I gathered that his patients were wealthy and felt they had to consult him every time they had so much as a twinge. With most of them, he got symptoms over the telephone, said he'd telephone a drugstore and have a prescription rushed right out. Two of them he promised to come and see. The rest of them he stalled off.

"That's the way it goes," he said when he'd finished the calls and hung up the telephone. "I'll go make those calls. It'll take about an hour. Want to wait here, or come with me?"

"I'll wait here."

"Look around," he said. "My wife will give you every co-operation."

"Those two calls?" I asked. "Are they really urgent?"

For a moment, there was a grimace of distaste on his

12

face. "Hell, no," he said. "But they're regular patients who demand service. A bunch of damn neurotics who sit up playing bridge until after midnight every night, keep guzzling food into their stomachs, drink too damn much liquor, don't get any exercise, are overweight, and past fifty. When you get that combination, you're headed for trouble."

"Nothing the matter with them?" I asked.

"Sure, there's plenty the matter with them," he said. "Their blood pressures are high. Their arteries are caked up. Their hearts are going bad. Their kidneys are breaking down. It never occurs to them they have any responsibility in connection with their own health. When something goes wrong with one of their cars, they call the garage mechanic to come and fix it. When they get one of nature's warnings, they call me as their body mechanic to come out and fix 'em up."

"What do you do? Give them a diet and—"

"Diet, hell! They'd get another doctor tomorrow if I suggested *they* do anything. They want *me* to do it. And how the hell are you going to watch your food when you're eating four or five dinners a week that are social ceremonies? I can't do it myself, and my patients can't—and won't. I treat the symptoms, give them hypnotics, tell 'em that if they'll stay in bed tomorrow morning, there's no reason they can't go to Mrs. What-You-May-Call-Her's shindig tomorrow night, and—say, why the hell am I telling you all this?"

"Because I wanted to know."

His voice got cold all at once. "Confine your curiosity to finding Miss Starr," he said. "I'll take care of my medical practice."

When he had his hand on the knob of the door, I said, "Well, I know who has the jewelry. It isn't Miss Starr."

"Who is it?"

"You."

I noticed then that the flesh around his eyes was so puffy he couldn't get them really wide open. He was trying hard enough. "Me!" he said.

"That's right."

"You're crazy!"

I said, "No. It's a pretty safe bet. The jewel robbery just couldn't have happened the way you say it did. You've given the police a description of the jewelry. They'll get it back if it's pawned. A thousand is too much to pay for a reward, and you offered it too easily.

"My guess is there was something in that safe you valued very highly. You found it was missing. You had to find out who had it. You couldn't resort to ordinary means. So you got your wife to give you her jewelry to put in the safe. You put the jewelry in all right, then you opened the safe and took it out, and called the police the next day. In that way, you put pressure on whoever had taken the thing you wanted. Nollie Starr couldn't stand the pressure. When she realized you'd planted the jewel robbery, she knew she was licked. That told you all you wanted to know. Now you want to talk with Miss Starr."

He closed the door and came back toward me, walking slowly, ominously, as though he intended to hit me. When he was within two steps of my chair, he stopped and said, "Lam, that's preposterous."

I said, "After all, I'm here to help you. You can't help a patient if he lies to you about his symptoms. I can't help you unless you tell me the truth. It isn't the jewels you want from Miss Starr, is it?"

He said, "Well, your reasoning is all wet. You find Miss Starr and get the jewels back. Then you're through. Just confine yourself to that and—and don't make so many deductions."

He looked at his watch, said, "I have to see those two patients. I've got to stop at the drugstore to rush out some prescriptions. You sit right here in the study. You'll find some interesting reading in that diathermy machine. I'll tell you the low-down when I return."

"Which is the diathermy machine?"

"The one over here to the left of that easy chair. Sit down, turn on the light, and read."

"When will you be back?"

He looked at his watch again, and said, "I'll be back by nine o'clock—nine-thirty at the latest. And don't go making any more deductions. Don't talk with anyone. Sit here and read." He turned and walked rapidly out of the study. I had the impression he was glad to get away.

chapter 2

IN THE SPRING AND LATE FALL, southern California has peculiarly violent desert windstorms, known as "santanas," sometimes called "Santa Anas." For hours before such winds start, the sky will be clear and dustless. The details of objects miles away can be seen with startling clarity. The air will be warm, listless, devoid of life. Silk or rayon garments will crackle with static electricity.

Then suddenly a blast of wind comes sweeping down from the east and north, a hot, dry wind which churns particles of dust so fine they filter between dry lips, grit against the surfaces of teeth. As a rule, those storms blow for three days and three nights. Those sections which are protected from the wind itself nevertheless feel the dehydrating effects of the dry, hot air. People's nerves get raw. They are listless and irritable. Perspiration is sucked up by the dry air so the hot skin becomes gritty with dust.

I sat in Dr. Devarest's study and did a little thinking. There was a balcony, and when the air became so close it seemed no windows in the room were open, I stepped out to this balcony.

One look at the star-studded sky, and I knew a santana was coming. Stars blazed down with such steady brilliance the heavens seemed filled to overflowing. The air out of

15

doors seemed as close as it was in the study—warm, dry, devitalizing air that made one's nerves stand on edge.

I went back to the study. The cabinet Dr. Devarest had indicated was an elaborate affair equipped with dials, switches, and indicators. A metal plate on the front bore the legend, *Continental Diathermy Laboratories, Inc. De Luxe Model AAA-6*. A little investigation showed me where there was a hinge and a catch on the side. I opened the little door. A recess beneath a tangle of wires was filled with books. I pulled out three or four, adjusted the reading-lamp, settled back, and started to read.

When I had finished the third chapter, the wind struck. It struck with the force of a solid wall. The house swayed with the force of that first terrific gust. All over the place I could hear doors slamming, could hear people running, and the sound of closing windows. The study was on the south and west side of the house, so the force of the wind did not sweep directly in through the windows, but it soon became necessary to close them because of the infiltration of fine dust that eddied in through the openings.

I went back to my book, and became interested in it. As is so frequently the case with a professional man who reads for relaxation, Dr. Devarest was a good judge of mysteries. This book made me think I was really working on the case. Time passed unnoticed.

Behind me a board creaked.

My nerves are always on edge during those windstorms. I dropped the book from me, jumped, and whirled.

Nadine Croy was standing there regarding me with her dark, apprehensive eyes. She smiled at the way I jumped. "Were you going to wait for the doctor?" she asked.

"Yes."

Her hesitation was the quiet contradiction of a well-bred woman. I looked at my watch. It was twenty minutes to eleven. I said, "He told me he'd be back by nine-thirty at the latest."

16

She said, "I know. He sometimes is very erratic—when he's making a night call and encounters an emergency. Mrs. Devarest thought perhaps you'd like to return in the morning."

"Would it inconvenience the family if I waited?"

She said, "We *can* arrange to put you up here—if you feel quite certain that's what the doctor wants."

"I don't know what *he* wants," I said. "I only know what *I* want. I've got to get to work. I want to get some more data from him. I want to wait until he comes in, then get started."

"Perhaps I could help you."

I was a bit dubious about that. She watched me for a moment, then closed the study door and said, "Sit down, Mr. Lam. Perhaps we can put a few cards on the table and understand each other better."

I sat down. More than ever I saw something in her eyes, some hint of tragedy. It seemed that she was dreading something. Perhaps it was just that her eyes were too big for her face. She said, "I'm sorry Dr. Devarest employed you."

I didn't say anything to that.

"Because," she said, after a brief pause, evidently for the purpose of drawing me out, "I know what you're after."

"The jewels?" I asked.

"The jewels," she said, and the way she said it was as though she had given a sniff of contempt. "You're after the things he had in his safe."

"Perhaps you know more than I do," I said.

I saw her eyelids droop just a bit as she considered the possibility of that suggestion; then she shook her head and said, "No. Dr. Devarest would have to take you into his confidence. You're after the things that were in that safe, the things that he tried to keep me from knowing about."

I kept quiet.

"You're not very talkative, are you?"

17

"There hasn't been anything to discuss so far."

"You might tell me whether my uncle has—been frank with you."

"That's something you'll have to discuss with the doctor."

"Have you found out anything about Miss Starr?"

"That's what I'm waiting for."

"Can you explain that a little?"

"I want to search her room. I want to check over the things she left behind."

"The police have been all through them."

"I know, but I want to look, anyway."

"Would you mind if *I* showed you?"

"Why not?"

"I don't know. You're holding yourself aloof as though—as though you'd been warned not to talk to me—or as though you suspected me of something."

I grinned at her. "I never pick my suspects until after I've found some evidence. So far I haven't even started to find the evidence."

She said, "Come on, then."

I put the book face down on the little smoking-stand by the chair, and followed her through Dr. Devarest's bedroom, down a long corridor, down a flight of back stairs, and into a wing at the back of the house. She opened the door of a room and said, "This is it."

The room was cheaply finished and furnished. Aside from that, it was neat, clean, and comfortable. There was a white-enameled iron bedstead, an ordinary pine dressing-table with a big mirror, a large bureau, a chest of drawers, a closet, a washstand above which was a little medicine cabinet, one rather dilapidated-looking overstuffed leather chair, a small table with a desk light, three straight-backed chairs, a small night stand by the side of the bed, and a cheap alarm clock that had a very audible metallic tick, a steady nerve-wracking *click—clack—click—clack.*

"Who wound the clock?" I asked.

"What do you mean?"

"Miss Starr left yesterday."

"Yes, yesterday afternoon."

"It's a twenty-four-hour clock, isn't it?"

"I don't know. I guess so, yes."

"Even if she'd wound it yesterday morning, it should have run down by this time."

She said vaguely, "I don't know. The police have been in here. They might have wound it."

I picked up the clock, and tried winding it. It was just about run down. The alarm had been turned to silent. The dial showed it was set for six-fifteen.

"Would you like to look around?" she asked.

I said, "Yes."

Mrs. Croy seemed dubious for a moment as to whether to leave me alone, then drew up a chair and sat down, watching me as I prowled around through the closet and the various drawers. "The police have been all through those things," she said again.

"I know. I'm looking for the things they missed."

"Such as what?" she asked.

I held up a pair of women's pigskin driving-gloves. "Such as these."

"What about them?"

I took the gloves over to the little desk light. "Notice anything about them?" I asked.

"No."

I took a handkerchief from my pocket, held it tightly over my forefinger, ran it across the fingers of the gloves, showed her the grease stain on the handkerchief.

She frowned. "Well?" she asked.

"Graphite grease," I said. "It has its uses, but it isn't as common as ordinary cup grease. These are her gloves?"

"Why, I don't know—I guess so. They were there on the dresser, weren't they?"

19

"Yes."

"Then they must have been hers."

"Any idea how she could have got graphite grease on them?"

"No."

"It's fresh, you see. She must have been working around some sort of machinery within the last few days."

"Yes," Mrs. Croy said in a tone of voice which showed she still didn't get it, or else was trying to belittle the significance of my discovery.

"Did she own a car?" I asked.

"No. She used the streetcar to go uptown on her days off. When she was on the job and had occasion to go anywhere for Aunt Colette, the chauffeur drove her."

I said, "I notice some shorts and rubber-soled tennis shoes in the closet. There are half socks that smell of rubber and foot perspiration."

She laughed and said, "Miss Starr is athletic. She liked to play tennis whenever she could inveigle the chauffeur into playing a set with her."

"Did she have leisure time in which to play tennis?"

"Only in the mornings."

"What time did she start work?"

"Breakfast was at eight. Her duties began immediately afterward. She'd take the mail in to Aunt Colette. Aunt Colette would sip coffee, open mail, and dictate replies."

"The tennis, then, was before breakfast. That explains why the alarm clock was set at six-fifteen."

Mrs. Croy's eyes showed sudden interest. "Say, you *do* get things."

I didn't say anything to that.

I opened the medicine cabinet and looked in at the bottles, jars, and tubes. "This her toothbrush?"

She laughed and said, "Really, Mr. Lam, I can't identify her toothbrush. It's a toothbrush, and it's there. After all, what difference does it make?"

"Because *if* it's her toothbrush, it indicates that she left in very much of a hurry."

"Well, you don't need to worry about that. I can assure you she left in *very* much of a hurry. As you can see, she didn't even come back to her room—not long enough to take anything."

I pushed my hands down in my pockets and leaned back against the bureau, staring down at the painted floor.

"Well?" she asked. "What's so important? Really, Mr. Lam, conceding that you're a very skillful professional detective, you must admit the police aren't exactly stupid. They've been over this place in detail. I think you can rest assured they've found every important clue that's here."

"How about the clues that aren't here?" I asked.

"That's one of those enigmatic questions, isn't it?"

I didn't say anything. After a while, her curiosity impelled her to ask, "Hope I didn't hurt your feelings. What were you referring to?"

"When?"

"A minute ago when you said something about a clue that wasn't here."

"Not the clue that isn't here," I said. "But it's the thing that isn't here which may be a clue."

"What?"

"The tennis racket."

"What do you mean?"

I moved my hand in an inclusive gesture. "Apparently she left without returning to her room. She'd been playing tennis in the mornings. She'd evidently played tennis yesterday morning. One plays tennis with a tennis racket. A tennis racket is quite apt to be in a case with a zipper pocket containing some tennis balls. There isn't any tennis racket."

"Are you certain?"

"I've looked the place over. I don't see one."

There was perplexity in her eyes. "But she *has* a tennis

racket. I know she has one."

"Well, where is it?"

"I don't know. It seems—well, that certainly *is* strange."

We were silent for almost a minute. I could hear the *click-clack* of the alarm clock, and the sound of the wind whistling around the corners of the house, rustling the dry fronds of the palm trees outside the window. I was also conscious of some rhythmic undertone of sound which had been knocking at the door of my consciousness, demanding admission. But I'd been so engrossed trying to find some clue that I hadn't really noticed it. Now I stopped to listen. It was a steady, throbbing noise, such as might have been made by the motor in a big icebox—yet it had been running steadily.

"The kitchen near here?" I asked.

"Fairly near."

"I wonder if someone's left the door of the icebox open."

"Why?"

"That motor," I said. "It's been running steadily."

She listened, pursed her lips, said, "Let's go see."

I followed her from the bedroom, down a corridor, through a door, across a serving-pantry, and into a modern kitchen which glistened with white enamel and electrical efficiency. There was a huge icebox by the end of the sink. The door was closed. The motor was silent. From the kitchen we couldn't hear the sound of the motor.

"Let's go back and listen again," I suggested.

As we entered the corridor which ran the length of the wing containing the servants' bedrooms, I could hear the sound again. "Where's the garage?" I asked.

She pointed down toward the end of this wing. "The driveway runs along here, right past these windows."

I listened more carefully. "Let's go take a look. Can we get through here?"

"Yes. There's a door from the back of this wing."

She led the way, switching on lights. She opened a door,

entered a tool room containing an assortment of wrenches, jacks, tires, and tools. The sound of the running motor was audible from here—just about the same as it had been from the bedroom. She opened another door which led to the garage. A blast of hot air, laden with the fumes of combustion, struck our nostrils. I gave one look, jerked back, took a deep breath, and sprinted for the doors. They were the kind that slide up with a counter-balanced weight holding them in place. I jerked up the one in front of the car in which the motor was running. It was a light club coupé with battered fenders and a finish which indicated it had been left out in the weather a good deal of the time.

The wind came in with a rush, clearing the place of fumes. I ran back to the body of Dr. Hilton Devarest, got my hands under his armpits, and started dragging him toward the open air. Nadine Croy came to help me.

I knew it was no use as soon as I got a good look at his face. I'd seen that peculiar color on men's faces before. It's that reddish death color which is associated with asphyxiation from carbon monoxide.

Dr. Devarest was dead as a mackerel.

chapter 3

DR. DEVAREST'S RESIDENCE was in an exclusive suburban neighborhood. The sound of sirens brought annoyed silhouettes to lighted windows; then, as more sirens came, the lighted windows vanished behind heavy drapes as the neighbors resolutely shut out what had happened from its bedrooms and drawing-rooms. Burglary had been bad enough, but now a whole procession of sirens was making the night hideous.

The fire department brought a Pulmotor. The police came swarming out. Newspaper reporters took flashlight photographs. A deputy coroner arrived and checked up on the automobile. The hood had been raised as though someone had been trying to make an adjustment on the engine. There was grease on Dr. Devarest's right hand—a very definite smear of dark grease. There was also an end wrench which had been thrust in the left-hand side pocket of Dr. Devarest's coat. His surgical instrument bag, which he usually kept in his car, was on the floor near where his body was found. The gasoline tank was about a quarter full. Apparently no one had heard Dr. Devarest drive in. From any evidence in the garage, there was no indication of how long he had been lying there.

The deputy coroner had me point out as nearly as I could the position of the body at the time I had found it. He raised up the turtleback in the car, and prowled around inside. A moment later, he brought out two rubberized cases containing tennis rackets.

I looked at Mrs. Croy, and warned her to silence by partially lowering the lid over my right eye.

The deputy coroner looked at the cases, said, "Humph," took out the tennis rackets, and looked them over. Both of them showed signs of having been well used. One of them was a heavy-bodied racket of about fifteen ounces with a good thick grip. The other was a light racket of a sort which would be used by a woman.

I gathered from the expression on the deputy's face as he turned the rackets over in his hand that he didn't know much about tennis, and the rackets meant but little to him. He put them back in their cases, tossed them back into the storage compartment in the rear of the car, and prowled around looking for something else. When he failed to find anything, he dropped the turtleback into position and twisted the handle to lock the catch.

The deputy prowled around the front of the car. A pair of expensive pigskin driving-gloves were on the seat. "Anybody recognize these?" he asked.

Mrs. Croy said, "They're Dr. Devarest's."

"He usually drives with gloves?"

"Yes."

The coroner said, "Humph!"

He tried the glove compartment on the car. It was locked. "Who's got a key for this?" he asked.

Mrs. Croy said, "The ignition key's in the lock on the car. Won't that open the glove compartment?"

The deputy grunted an acknowledgment of the suggestion, took out the key, looked at it for a moment, then fitted it to the lock in the glove compartment. The metal door dropped down on its hinges. A small light automatically turned on, illuminating the interior. I saw a small stack of jewel cases.

The deputy pulled them out, opened one of them. It was empty. "Anybody any idea what these are?" he asked.

Mrs. Croy couldn't keep the startled exclamation from her lips. The deputy looked at her curiously. "Well," he asked, "what's the matter?"

"Are—are they *all* empty?"

The deputy picked up one or two, shook them, snapped them open, said, "Yes, they're all empty—wait a minute. Here's one—" He took out a ring, a big square-cut emerald surrounded by diamonds.

"Any idea how this got there?" he asked Mrs. Croy.

She had complete control of herself now. She spoke with the precision of one who is watching her words carefully. "The jewel cases are very similar to those in which Aunt Colette—Mrs. Devarest—keeps her jewels. The ring which you are holding in your hand is, I am quite certain, a ring belonging to her."

"What's the stuff doing here?" the deputy asked.

"I'm sure I don't know."

One of the radio-car officers came forward and said, "Cripes, Joe, there's a report out on those jewels. The safe in Dr. Devarest's study was burgled sometime Monday night or Tuesday morning. We've got a description of the whole business. Wait a minute—" He pulled a notebook from his pocket, opened it, thumbed through the pages, said, "One square-cut three-carat emerald, surrounded by eight white flawless matched diamonds, mounted in platinum ring."

"That's the baby," the deputy coroner said.

The men exchanged significant glances. The radio-car officer turned to Mrs. Croy. "How'd this stuff get here?"

She said, "I don't know."

He turned to me. "Let's see. You're a private detective?"

"Right."

"What brought you out here?"

"Dr. Devarest. I was waiting for him to come back. He wanted me to check on some phases of the safe robbery."

"What phases?"

"He didn't say."

The officer said, "Let's go talk with Mrs. Devarest."

"Okay. Let me finish up here. Now, let's see. Your name's Lam, huh?"

"Right."

"Exactly where was the body when you discovered it?"

"Just where I showed you."

"Well, you didn't show me well enough. Anybody got a piece of chalk?"

No one produced a piece of chalk.

The coroner said, "I may have one." He opened a briefcase, fumbled around, brought out a piece of chalk, and said, "All right, now mark there on the floor right where the body was lying. Make a little diagram. Mark the position of his head, of his feet, and of his arms."

I marked out the outline on the cement floor.

While I was bent over, working on my outline, I saw a face appear at the crack of the partially open door that led to the tool house. It was a dark face, handsome in a full-lipped, sensual way. The eyes were watching me with eager interest. Apparently the man was about to come in, but he had checked himself, waiting to see what I was doing.

26

"You had no business moving that body until I got here," the deputy charged as I finished.

"I didn't know it was a body until after I'd moved it."

The coroner took the chalk from my hand, dropped it in his briefcase, said, "Don't anybody move this automobile. Don't touch it. Now I'm going to take the fingerprints of everyone here, just to check up on those jewel cases. After that, we'll go talk with Mrs. Devarest. You two better come along."

They took our fingerprints. The man who had been standing at the door of the tool shed wasn't there any longer. They labeled our fingerprints, then Mrs. Croy and I followed the officer and deputy coroner into the house.

Mrs. Devarest was in her bedroom. The maid said she was being attended by Dr. Gelderfield, a friend of Dr. Devarest's who had come over to do what he could. He was called in whenever Mrs. Devarest wasn't feeling well. Doctors didn't treat their own families, she explained garrulously, and as Dr. Gelderfield's father was sick, Dr. Devarest treated him, and Dr. Gelderfield returned the compliment by treating Mrs. Devarest.

Dr. Gelderfield came out to meet the deputy coroner. He was a tall, thin, square-jawed individual who used close-clipped, decisive speech to impress his listeners. After listening for a minute he broke in definitely, "Mrs. Devarest is not to be disturbed. She has had a terrific shock. I've just given her a hypo. You may ask her to identify this ring, and *that's all!*"

The officer and the detective entered the bedroom. The doctor said to Mrs. Croy, "You two can remain here," and then followed the others.

Mrs. Croy looked at me. "What do you make of it?"

"Of what?"

"Of—you know—everything. The jewel cases being found in that glove compartment."

"It might have been any one of a number of things."

27

"What, for instance?"

"Oh, lots of things. One of those calls, you know, may have been from the thief who wanted to ransom the jewelry. The doctor might have given him the money, returned to the garage, and—"

"Then what happened to the jewelry?" she asked.

I said, "He'd been lying there for some time before we found him. Anyone could have opened the glove compartment by taking the ignition key out of the automobile."

She thought that over for a while and said, "You can't take the ignition key out with the motor running."

I said, "I'm not really trying to sell you the idea. I just brought it out for you to look at. It's something you can try on for size."

"Well, it doesn't fit."

"All right then, it doesn't fit."

The door from the bedroom opened. Dr. Gelderfield came out. "You're the detective?" he asked me.

"Yes."

"I mean the one Hilton hired?"

"Yes."

"Mrs. Devarest wants to see you. She's nervous and unstrung. She's suffered an intense shock. I've administered a hypodermic. It's commencing to take effect. Try to be brief. Don't argue with her. Just say something reassuring. It doesn't make any difference what it is."

"Lie?"

"Sure. Tell her anything. Relieve her mind. I want her to go to sleep."

"When do I go in?"

"As soon as those others come out." He frowned and said, "They were starting. Here they come now."

The deputy coroner and the radio-car officer came out of the bedroom. They were talking in low tones. They didn't seem even to notice Mrs. Croy and me. Dr. Gelderfield nodded his head in a silent gesture toward the door of the bedroom, and when Mrs. Croy started to follow me, motioned her back. I walked on in. Dr. Gelderfield came behind me and closed the door softly.

Mrs. Devarest was propped up in bed, three pillows behind her head and shoulders. She was wearing a blue negligee. Evidently the maid or Dr. Gelderfield, or both, had undressed her in a hurry. Her stockings were on the floor, her clothes on a chair. A corsetlike girdle which laced with soiled pink strings was draped over the back of the chair. It wasn't the way Colette Devarest would have liked to receive masculine visitors.

Her pop eyes looked at me as though they were having trouble in focusing. Her voice sounded a little fuzzy.

She said, "What's your name again?"

"Lam. Donald Lam."

"Oh, yes—I'd forgotten. It was a shock." Her eyelids fluttered closed, then snapped open again. "I want you to keep right on."

"With what?"

"The investigation. You know what those men intimated?"

"What?"

"That Hilton had stolen the jewels. . . . He didn't. . . . It's imperative that his name be vindicated. . . . He didn't have any financial worries—making good money—forty thousand dollars in insurance—double in case of accidental death. . . . You'll fix everything up for me, won't you, Mr.— what's your name again?"

"Lam."

"Won't you, Mr. Lam?"

"I'll get on the job," I told her.

"Come and see me in the morning, will you?"

"If you wish."

"I do."

"What time?"

"After breakfast."

"Not before ten-thirty," Dr. Gelderfield said in crisp, professional accents.

She rolled her eyes toward him. Her voice was sounding thick now. "You want me to sleep, don't you, Warren?"

"Yes."

I said, "Go right ahead and get some sleep, Mrs. Devarest. Our agency will get on the job. We'll work day and night. There's nothing for you to worry about. Just lie back and take it easy."

Dr. Gelderfield slipped some of the pillows out from behind her head. "That's the best thing to do, Colette. Let this young man work on it. Now, you've fixed that up, and you can dismiss it from your mind. Just let it go."

"Just let it go," she repeated drowsily.

Dr. Gelderfield motioned to me.

I tiptoed from the room.

Mrs. Croy was waiting for me. "What did she want?" she asked quickly.

"Wanted me to come back at ten-thirty in the morning."

For a moment there was a flash of anger in her dark eyes. "Aren't you funny?" she said, and turned away.

chapter 4

THE ALARM WENT OFF at quarter to six. I was drugged with sleep. It took a cold shower to sting me awake. I shaved, dressed, went down to the garage, got out the agency car, and started a round of the municipal parks. It was a tedious business, but there wasn't much traffic, so I could get around fairly easily. The desert wind had quit during the night. The crisp feel of early morning was in the air. While the sun was up, it wasn't as yet hot. Even down in the concrete canyons of the city streets the air seemed filled with freshness, sharp contrast to what would happen during the next few hours when the sun softened the pavement and the lifeless air became filled with exhaust gases.

30

Out at the parks, there were a few scattered tennis players. Some of them were women, attired in shorts. They looked at me curiously as I drove slowly past the courts.

It wasn't until I got out to Griffith Park that I saw a mixed foursome playing. One of the girls interested me. She was as full of life as a steel spring. When she was serving, she'd toss up the ball, arch back her powerful body, then throw everything she had into an overhead smash which sent the serve whizzing across the net. When the ball struck, it sailed into a long, powerful bounce that, on the first serve, all but knocked the racket out of the hands of her masculine opponent. He got on to her delivery after a couple of serves, and started smashing them back at her. That was only one of the things which convinced me he hadn't played with her before.

She slowed her serves down for her feminine opponent, and I realized the two girls were strangers.

The girl in whom I was interested evidently knew the man who was her partner. He was a good consistent player, a little too inclined to be conservative. A bicycle leaned up against the wire fence, a sweater strapped to the handle bars.

I parked my car, switched off the motor, lit a cigarette, and watched.

They quit about seven forty-five. There was a little conversation across the net, the sort of "Well, you gave us a nice game" stuff, and "Glad we happened to run onto you. We'll try it again some morning. We should have a chance at revenge, but you were too powerful for us."

After a while, the girl came out of the tennis court, unstrapped the sweater from the handle bars, slipped it on, and wrapped a button skirt around the shorts of her play suit. I went over and raised my hat.

She looked at me with cold, uninterested eyes. She certainly wasn't a pickup.

"Nice game you play," I said.

31

"Thank you," she said in a voice which wasn't exactly cold, but was certainly distant.

"Don't go away," I said.

Her glance was scornful.

"I'd like to talk with you, Miss Starr."

She was just ready to put her foot down on the pedal when I mentioned her name. She stopped all motion and looked at me curiously.

"Sorry to take this unconventional method of getting acquainted, but I had to see you before you saw the morning papers."

She was studying me now with eyes so cautious and expressionless they might have been enameled with an airbrush—the tannish gray color that is used so frequently on automobiles. "Who are you?" she asked.

I gave her one of the agency cards. She looked it over and asked, "What's in the morning papers?"

I said, "Dr. Devarest was found dead in his garage. Carbon monoxide."

She locked her feelings behind the mask of a frozen face. "Trying to get my goat?" she asked.

"Trying to tell you the truth."

"How did you find me?"

"Not many girls in the city who are tennis enthusiasts ride a bicycle to the tennis courts and play early in the morning."

"How did you know I did that?"

"Your gloves—graphite grease from the chain of a bicycle. A young woman who is as much of a tennis enthusiast as you probably played tennis on her days off. That meant you had a second racket which you kept in your room, or apartment. You didn't have an automobile. You'd been working for Mrs. Devarest about three months. Your other tennis racket, you know, was found by the police in the back of Dr. Devarest's automobile."

She said, "Poor man, he had Bright's disease—and lots

32

of courage. For years he'd been noting his own symptoms, doing virtually nothing to take care of himself, keeping notes on the progress of the disease. I felt if I could get him out early in the morning, I might do something with him. He always felt he had no chance to get outdoor exercise because he was on call; but I pointed out that patients almost never called early in the morning. Their favorite time is at night right after a doctor has gone to sleep."

"And in order to keep Mrs. Devarest from being jealous, he told her that he had early morning calls?"

She shrugged her shoulders and said, "I don't know what he told her. We only played a few times. Is that on the square about—about what happened to him?"

"Yes."

"How did it happen?"

"Apparently he'd driven his car into the garage. Something was wrong with the motor, and he wanted to adjust it, or connect a loose wire somewhere."

She said slowly, "He was a great hand to tinker around with his automobile—spark plugs and things of that sort."

"How about that chauffeur?"

"Dr. Devarest hated to be waited on. He liked to do things for himself. He wouldn't let a chauffeur drive him anywhere. The chauffeur was for Mrs. Devarest. She used him as a sort of lackey."

"And why did you leave as soon as the safe was robbed?"

She said, "That's neither here nor there," and started to get on her wheel.

I said, "Right now, it's here. Within a very short time, it's going to be there. Your disappearance drew suspicion to you. The police are going to find you."

She got off her wheel, parked it up against the heavy wire mesh of the tennis court, and said, "All right, let's talk. Shall I get in your automobile?"

I nodded.

I held the door open for her. She said, "Go ahead and

slide in. I'll get in beside you."

I slid over behind the steering-wheel, and she came up beside me with a quick, lithe motion. "You ask questions," she inquired, "or do I talk?"

"You talk," I said.

"Got a cigarette?"

I gave her one. She lit it and settled her shoulders back against the cushion of the seat. I could see she was sparring for a little time. I didn't hurry her any, but let her smoke and think.

She said, "It goes back a ways."

"What does?"

"The reason I left."

"How far back?"

"Quite a little while."

"Something on the job?"

"No, no. Something that happened a long time before that. That's why I took the name of Starr, and started out on my own."

"What was it that happened?"

"Something that I wanted to forget about and wanted others to forget about."

"What was it?"

"We won't go into that."

"If I knew, I might be able to help you."

"I don't need any help."

"That's what you think. You're in a spot."

"How so?"

"Jewels vanish. Secretary vanishes. Police don't have a great deal of imagination. They put two and two together, and, in that arrangement, it always makes at least four, sometimes six or eight. In this instance, perhaps twelve."

"If they find me, we'll see if we can't correct their addition."

"I found you."

"Are you the police?"

34

"No."

"What then?"

"Just an investigator."

"Employed by whom?"

"Dr. Devarest."

"For what purpose?"

"To find you."

"All right, now you've found me. So what?"

"I'll have to report to my client."

"He's dead."

"His wife."

She shook her head, said, "No, you don't. I get out of this automobile, get on my bicycle, and ride away."

"Suppose I don't see things that way?"

"What could you do about it?"

"Take you down to the nearest police station."

"I'd require a lot of taking."

"I'd require a lot of escaping from."

"But you don't want to turn me over to the police?"

"Those weren't my instructions. I think the doctor was more interested in finding you than in finding the jewels."

She looked me over pretty carefully for several seconds. "Just what do you mean by that crack?"

"There was something in the safe that he wanted. He thought that the person who opened the safe wanted it, too. Taking the jewels was just a blind. If the jewels were taken at all. That may have been just a gag he thought up so he could call in the police."

"And he thought I got what was in the safe?"

"Apparently."

"I haven't got it."

I said, "I was hired to find you. I've found you. You can talk it over with my clients."

"Look here, Mrs. Devarest isn't your client."

I grinned and said, "She's inherited me."

"Do you know what was in that safe?"

"No."

She smoked for a few moments, either debating whether to tell me, or else trying to think up a good lie. Then she ground out the end of the cigarette in the ash tray, and said, "Dr. Devarest worshiped the ground Nadine Croy walked on, not only for her sake, but because of the little girl, Selma. He would have done anything to have protected their happiness."

She paused and looked me over. "Did he tell you anything about that?"

"This is your show," I said. "I'm just the audience. Keep the act moving."

"You mean you wouldn't tell me if he had?"

"No."

"Would you tell me if he hadn't?"

"No. The things I know I'm keeping to myself so I can check that much of your story."

She said, "I don't know exactly what it was. Walter Croy, Nadine's husband, is a prize heel. He'd been bothering Nadine. He wanted custody of Selma, at least part of the time. He had lawyers, and a lot of petitions to the court, and even some affidavits about a cocktail party Nadine went to. Then all of a sudden, everything quit. We didn't hear anything more from Walter. And about that time the doctor had this wall safe installed."

"Any other evidence beside that?" I asked.

"Yes."

"What?"

"Just little things, little comments."

"You think Dr. Devarest had something to do with Walter Croy's laying off of Nadine?"

"Yes."

"What?"

"I don't know. Dr. Devarest had the whip hand in some way. I guess you couldn't call it blackmail, but it was something."

"Interesting," I said.

"Isn't it?"

"And so when the safe was burgled, you took a powder?"

"That's right."

"And had a game of tennis afterward with the doctor?"

"After what?"

"After you'd taken the powder."

"No. That was before."

"Oh, you *did* play tennis with him then?"

"I told you that."

"But you didn't say you'd played tennis with him Wednesday morning."

"Not Wednesday. Tuesday. He was going fishing Wednesday. I left Tuesday afternoon."

"Where are you living?"

"That's my business."

"You want me to go to Mrs. Devarest with a story like that?"

"No. If you've got good sense, you'll keep your mouth shut. You'll go to Mrs. Devarest and say, 'Look, your husband's unfortunate death terminated my employment. I don't suppose *you* care about going ahead and paying me money to find your jewels. On the other hand, Dr. Devarest had made a definite contract. Suppose we call it quits? You pay me some cash by way of compromise, and I walk out on the case.'"

"Why should I do that?"

"Because everyone will be happier that way."

I said, "The doctor evidently thought you had what he wanted—whatever came out of that safe."

She said, "No. You've got that wrong. The doctor thought I knew who had it."

"Do you?"

She hesitated for a second or two, then said, "No."

"Could you make a good guess?"

"No."

"If Dr. Devarest had been alive, you wouldn't have said no to both those questions quite as quickly, would you?"

She raised her eyes to mine. "Why not?"

I said, "I wish I knew the answer to that myself."

"I could use another cigarette," she said.

I gave her one. I could tell, from the way she lit it, she was doing a lot of thinking. Abruptly, she said, "Look, I've got to take a shower, and get some breakfast. You don't want to turn me over to the police. You don't intend to let me get away. Suppose I make a deal with you? Suppose I tell you where I'm living, and we let it go at that?"

"Where?"

"The Bel Aire. That's only a few blocks from here, down Vermont."

"Living by yourself?"

"No. I share an apartment with another girl."

"You also had a room at Dr. Devarest's?"

"Yes. My duties kept me there, but I had a day off, and that meant two nights."

"When was your day off?"

"Wednesdays. I'd leave the house Tuesday night and get back Thursday morning."

I said, "Let's see. Dr. Devarest was taking it easier, too. Wasn't he? I believe he was trying to take Wednesdays off."

She looked at me coldly. "Is that intended to be a crack or are you just trying to draw me out?"

"Which one would work the better?"

"Neither," she said, and determinedly pushed the handle on the door. I let her get out. She walked over to the bicycle, climbed on, and pedaled rapidly down the drive without even looking back. I stayed behind, keeping her in sight. She went to the Bel Aire Apartments, dismounted, parked the bicycle at the pavement, and walked in.

I found a parking place for the car, found a telephone, and called Elsie Brand, Bertha's efficient, taciturn secretary. "Had breakfast, Elsie?"

"Just finished."

"Got time to do a job?"

"What?"

"Smash a bicycle."

"With what?"

"Your private automobile. It's an agency job."

"Does Bertha know about it?"

"No."

"Better call her, hadn't you?"

"No. It would take too long to explain."

"Where are you?"

"Parked at the curb a few doors down the street from the Bel Aire Apartments on Vermont."

She said, "Can I do it and still get uptown in time to open the office?"

"I think so. It shouldn't take long."

"Exactly what do I do?"

I said, "Get this straight. Take the side street to the corner northwest of the Bel Aire. Toot your horn twice as you come around the corner into Vermont. Slow almost to a stop to give me a little time. I'll drive away. There's a bicycle parked in front of the apartment house. If it isn't there when you get here or if you don't see me drive away when you toot, just go open up the office and forget about it."

"All right," she said, "I toot. You're there. You drive away. The bicycle is there. Then what do I do?"

"Try parking your car in close to the apartment house. You're not very smart at parking, and you smash the bicycle, smash it good enough so it can't be ridden away."

"Then what?"

"A girl in a play suit will come out and get indignant."

"What do I do?"

"You're insured with the Auto Club, aren't you?"

"Yes."

"Get very haughty. Tell her that she had no business

39

leaving her bicycle there in the first place, that you're insured with the Auto Club, and that you really can't be bothered with little things. Give her your name and address, then drive away."

"That's all?"

"That's all."

"Don't try to follow her?"

"Absolutely not. Not under any circumstances."

"Then what?"

"Report to the Auto Club and tell them that when she makes a claim for damages, you want to see all the details."

"Okay," she said, "on my way."

I hung up and went back to wait in the automobile. I thought Elsie Brand could probably get there in ten minutes if she hurried. That was one nice thing about Elsie. If she was going to do anything, she did it very thoroughly and very efficiently.

She made it in exactly eight and one-half minutes from the time I hung up the telephone. I heard her toot the horn as she came around the corner, got a glimpse of her car in my rear-view mirror. I ostentatiously looked at my watch, scribbled a note in my notebook, and drove away, trying to look very smug and self-satisfied.

Driving straight down Vermont, I looked back through my rear-view mirror. I could see Elsie Brand inching her car in toward a parking place, then I saw the front wheel turn sharply, and the car smash into the parked bicycle.

There was a street intersection ahead, and I turned the car to the right.

chapter 5

I HAD A LEISURELY BREAKFAST and went up to the office. Elsie Brand was clacking away on her typewriter as I came in. Her fingers kept hammering at the keyboard as she looked up to give me a quick nod.

"Everything okay?" I asked.

"Uh huh."

"Girl came out?"

"Yes."

"Where's the boss?"

"Inside. Reading the paper."

I went on in. Bertha was seated at the big desk. Her ocean fishing was making her brown as Shredded Wheat. Her flowing white hair gave her a motherly appearance. "Reading about Dr. Devarest?" I asked.

"Yes. How did it happen, Donald?"

"He told me to wait in his study, said he'd be back by nine-thirty at the latest. I got interested reading a book and didn't realize how fast time was passing."

"The newspaper says you discovered the body."

"That's right."

She made a little grimace and said, "I guess that winds up the case. Just when it looked as though Bertha had a nice piece of business, too."

I said, "I think Mrs. Devarest is going to want us. I've found the Starr girl."

"You have?"

"Uh huh."

"How'd you do it?"

"Oh, just a little leg work. I found she rode a bicycle and played tennis early in the mornings. I had a pretty fair description. There aren't many women who ride bicycles to tennis courts early in the morning."

"Where is she now?"

"I don't know."

Bertha scowled. "What do you mean by that?"

"I couldn't follow her, not when she knew I was on the job. She gave me a phony address—the Bel Aire Apartments. She rode the bicycle up there and went in. She'd have waited there until I drove away. I didn't want to inconvenience her, so I drove away."

"Couldn't you have followed her?"

"Ever try following a good rider on a bicycle with an automobile?"

She thought that over.

I said, "She'd have gone out into heavy traffic, taken a street that had two lanes of automobiles waiting for a signal, slipped out in between the lanes, and left me sitting there with the motor running."

"What did you do?"

"Got Elsie to smash the bicycle. Elsie is insured with the Automobile Club."

"Think the girl will be sucker enough to make a claim under her right name?"

"I think so. Elsie can put on a good act. I told her to be snooty and disinterested, mention the Auto Club, and drive away."

"What about Mrs. Devarest?"

"I'm to see her at ten-thirty."

"What's she want?"

"The police think her husband may have stolen the gems himself. She wants his name cleared."

"Can you do it?"

"No."

"Why?"

"Because he stole them."

Bertha studied me with her little, hard eyes. She took a cigarette from the humidor on the desk, inserted one end in a long, carved ivory holder, lit it, and sat there trying to think of something to say. The diamonds on her left hand flashed as she raised the cigarette holder once more to her mouth.

"What did you tell her?"

"I told her I'd take the job."

"Why did you tell her that, if you think he stole them?"

"Because her doctor said that I wasn't to disturb her."

"But you're going out there at ten-thirty?"

"Yes."

"I don't get you."

I said, "Mrs. Devarest dropped an interesting remark."

"What?"

"She said her husband carried forty thousand dollars in insurance, that the policies paid double in case of accidental death."

"Well, what about it?"

"Insurance policies don't read that way."

"Bosh!" Bertha said. "I have one myself. Ten thousand payable to my estate. That'll clean up my bills. In case I meet an accidental death, it pays twenty."

"No, it doesn't."

Bertha flushed. "Do you mean to say I don't know what my own insurance policy says?"

"Yes."

Bertha carefully laid down the carved ivory cigarette holder. She opened a drawer, took out some keys, opened another drawer, unlocked a box, took out a life insurance policy, folded it over, and said, "Read it."

I looked over her shoulder.

"Well," Bertha said triumphantly.

"You're wrong."

"What!"

"You're wrong."

"You're crazy! Here it is, just as I said. It's right here in black and white."

"No. It isn't. This policy pays double in case the death is by accidental means."

"Well, what did I tell you?"

"You said accidental death."

"What's the difference?"

I said, "Try to collect from an insurance company, and you'll find out the difference."

Bertha kept looking at me. She said, "Sometimes, Donald, I love you, and sometimes I hate your damn guts." She folded the policy, put it back in the box, locked the box, closed the drawer, dropped the keys in the other drawer of the desk. After a while she said, "All right, you studied law. You know the answers. I'm dumb. Personally, the way I look at that policy, if I meet with an accidental death, my estate gets twenty thousand."

I said, "There's a difference between an accidental death and a death by accidental means. In one case, your death is the result of an accident. You do something, and because of something you overlooked, you die. That's an accidental death. In order to make it a death by accidental means, there must be something in the very means of death which is accidental."

Bertha said, "I don't get it."

I said, "If you drive into a garage and start tinkering with your car, leave the motor running, inhale carbon monoxide, and die, there's nothing accidental about the *means* of your death. All of the means were set in motion by you. You started the engine. You were negligent. You stayed in the poisoned atmosphere too long."

"And under those circumstances she wouldn't get twice the face of the policy?"

"That's right."

Bertha said, "How did you know her policy is the same as mine?"

"They're all the same—all I've ever seen. It's a standard form."

"Don't the insurance companies know the difference?"

"They do. They're about the only ones who do. Lots of lawyers don't even know the difference."

Bertha said, "What are you going to do?"

"Just keep stalling along until the insurance company breaks the bad news to Mrs. Devarest."

"Then what?"

"Then I'll let her go see her lawyer."

"Then what?"

"Then when all the others have given up, I'll suggest

44

we can collect the other forty thousand dollars for her—the double-benefit clause."

"How?"

"I don't know—yet."

"If we collect forty thousand for her, we should get half, and—"

I said, "Be reasonable."

"Well, we should get something substantial out of it."

"We should."

Bertha said suddenly, "I mean I should. I would, of course, give you a nice bonus, and—"

"*We* should," I said.

Bertha frowned. "What are you getting at?"

I said, "I'm quitting."

The springs creaked on Bertha Cool's chair as she came swinging up in straight-backed indignation. "You're doing what!" she demanded, her voice harsh.

"Quitting."

"When?"

"Right now."

"For what?"

"I'm getting a full partnership in a business."

"What business?"

"A detective agency."

"Whose?"

"Yours."

Bertha thought that over.

"You need to do more fishing," I explained.

She said, "Donald, you're a brainy little cuss. You've got lots of imagination and daring. It would bother Bertha to have to get along without you, but you haven't any business ability. You throw money to the birdies. This place would go broke in six months if I took you in the partnership. Now you let Bertha run the finances, and she'll give you a bonus on—"

"A full partnership or nothing."

"All right then," she snapped angrily, "it's nothing. I'm not going to be held up. I—"

"Take it easy," I told her. "Don't lose your temper. Tell Elsie to make out a check for what I've got coming."

"How about your appointment with Mrs. Devarest?"

"You can go out and keep it."

Bertha pushed back her chair. Her face was mottled with anger. "By God, I will!"

"Be careful not to excite her," I said. "The doctor doesn't want her excited. Excitement is bad for the arteries. Anger is the worst of all."

I told my landlady I was going to San Francisco to look for work, that my rent was paid until the first. If I couldn't get back to move things out by the first, I'd arrange to have someone pack and ship my things.

She'd never approved of me, but she was sorry to lose me. I was regular pay, and had steady work. She wanted to know why I'd been discharged. I told her I hadn't been discharged, I'd quit. I could see she didn't believe it.

I went to San Francisco, stayed for three days at a cheap hotel, and on the third day wrote my landlady on the hotel stationery that I'd decided to remain in San Francisco permanently.

The next morning I went out to breakfast, then went out to the beach and did some ice skating. I had lunch, sat around out on the beach until the fog began to roll in, then went back uptown to a movie. I got back to the hotel about five o'clock.

Bertha Cool was sitting in the lobby. She was so mad her eyes were snapping.

"Where the hell have you been?" she demanded.

"Oh, just looking around," I said. "How is everything?"

"Rotten."

"That's too bad. Been waiting long?"

"You know damn well I have. I came up on the plane.

46

I got here at quarter past twelve, and I've been sitting in this lobby ever since."

I said, "That's too bad. Why didn't you go to your hotel and leave a message for me to call you?"

"Because you wouldn't have called," she snapped. "And anyway, I wanted to talk with you before you had a chance to—to—"

"Think things over," I finished.

Bertha said, "Where is there a cocktail bar around here?"

"A couple of blocks down the street."

"All right, let's go."

San Francisco's invigorating fog gave the air a snappy tang. Bertha Cool, with her chin up, her shoulders back, strode along the street with a lusty swing to her legs and shoulders. She was so mad she couldn't even see where she was going. Twice in the two blocks she started to plow through intersection signals. I had to grab her arm to keep her from getting run over or arrested.

We settled down in a cocktail bar. Bertha ordered a double brandy. I had Scotch and soda. Bertha said over the drink, "Well, you called the turn."

"On what?"

"On everything," she admitted. "The insurance people were very, very sympathetic. They couldn't pay the double indemnity because the death wasn't by accidental *means,* but they didn't want to keep the widow from getting her money right away. They kept waving a check for forty thousand under her nose. They told her she could accept it without prejudicing her rights to sue for the other forty —if she wanted to. They suggested she go see a lawyer."

"Then what?"

"She went to see her lawyer. Her lawyer told her she was licked before she started. There's a rumor now that Dr. Devarest had robbed his own safe and that he committed suicide when he thought they were going to catch up with him. He was a sick man, anyway."

"Tell me more about that suicide theory."

"Well, there wasn't anything on the motor which needed fixing. It was running like a clock. There weren't any of his fingerprints on the wrench or on anything on the motor—only on the hood. It looks as though he tried to take the easy way out, and spare his wife's feelings by making it look like an accident."

"Find the Starr girl?" I asked.

"She didn't make a claim at the Auto Club. And I—well, I haven't done anything about it."

"Why?"

"I don't think Mrs. Devarest wants to find her particularly."

"Why not?"

"I think that girl and the doctor—well, there was something between them."

"Who told you so?"

"Mrs. Devarest. She'd been picking up a little gossip. She said that it would be a lot better to let bygones be bygones. The funeral was yesterday."

"That's interesting, isn't it?" I asked.

She said, "Damn you!"

I raised my eyebrows. "What's the matter?"

She said, "I've been to the best lawyers in the city. I've paid out fifty dollars for two legal opinions, twenty-five dollars a shot."

"Did you indeed? Why? I don't get it."

Bertha Cool said, "The lawyers looked up the decisions, went over the facts carefully, and said Mrs. Devarest hasn't a leg to stand on. Even if the death wasn't suicide, but was accidental, it wasn't by accidental *means*, just the way you pointed out. Mrs. Devarest has seen her own lawyer. He thought at first she had a case, then after he looked it up, he said she didn't. Mrs. Devarest would pay half of that forty thousand to collect it."

"Is that so?"

Bertha flared into indignation. "Locked away in the ball-bearing brain of yours is some scheme by which she could collect that money. I'll bet she'd give seventy-five per cent of it to collect it. She's so mad at the insurance people. Dr. Devarest always thought the policy provided for accidental death. She did, too. The insurance people are nice and sympathetic. They're *so* sorry. They'd like to pay off—if they could. But you see it's a standard policy used by insurance people everywhere. They can't pay off under the circumstances. It'd be illegal."

I finished my Scotch and soda. "You know, San Francisco is a grand place," I said. "I think I'm going to like it."

"Like it, hell!" Bertha said. "You're coming back to pull this chestnut out of the fire for me."

"No. I've got a pretty good prospect up here, and—"

"You're coming back with Bertha," she said firmly. "I must have been crazy to let you go. I've grown to depend on you so much, I can't run the business without you."

I said, "No, Bertha, I don't think you'd be happy in a full partnership. You wouldn't get along well with a partner. You're too much of an individualist. You're too accustomed to having your own way. You like to carry the power of decision around with you."

Bertha said grimly, "That's where I'm going to fool you. I've thought this thing all out. This is *your* proposition. I'm going to take you up on it, and there's going to be one condition."

"What?"

"I'm going to be free to come and go as I please. You can hire anyone you want to do the work. I'm going to keep on fishing."

"Why the sudden love for the fish?" I asked.

"Thinking about Dr. Devarest," she said. "I went to his funeral. The poor guy had worked day and night. His nose had worn a groove in the grindstone. If he'd taken life a little easier, had relaxed once in a while, done a little more fishing, he'd have lived a lot longer. If he could have looked ahead, he'd have let some of those rich patients of his go jump in the lake, while he spent more time in the open.

"I used to be too fat to take any exercise. I felt like the devil all the time, but I was always ravenously hungry. Then I got sick and lost that weight, and when I got my strength back, I found I got a kick out of outdoor exercise. Now, I'm hard as nails, eat what I want to, and am holding my weight right where it is. You're young. You're naturally light. You don't have to worry about getting fat. You're going to stay in there and work. Bertha is going to fish. Now then, do you want that partnership or don't you?"

I grinned at her and said, "You may as well pay for the drinks, Bertha, because as a partner I'd put it on the expense account, anyway."

Bertha stared at me with hard, glittering eyes. She said, "You little devil! That's just what you *would* do, too!"

"It's exactly what I'm going to do from now on," I told her. "We may as well understand it at the start."

Bertha almost threw her purse in my face. She'd reconciled herself to the partnership idea, but the thought of having me buy drinks and put them on an expense account was the last straw.

"You know me," I said soothingly. "I haven't any idea of the value of money. I go around tossing it to the birdies."

Bertha glowered at me for what seemed like thirty seconds, then she took a deep breath, slowly and reluctantly opened her purse, took out a five-dollar bill, and called, "Oh, waiter!" To me she said, "If I pay for it myself, I'll at least save fifty per cent on the tip."

"*We* will," I corrected.

Her hard little eyes snapped angrily, but she didn't say anything.

chapter 6

MRS. DEVAREST SAID, "I'm glad you're back on the job, Mr. Lam. Of course, I like your partner, but somehow I have more confidence in you. Perhaps it was because Hilton picked you out."

She was dressed in black. Her face was without make-up, and her pop eyes seemed particularly mournful.

"Exactly what do you want done?" I asked.

She said, "Mrs. Cool said that you could find a way to make the insurance company pay that double indemnity clause."

I explained. "Insurance companies are regulated by law. They can't pay out on those claims unless the facts show a clear liability."

"I found that out," she said.

"I wouldn't want to try it unless everything else had failed."

"Well, everything's failed. Look here, Mr. Lam, I'll give you one half of any amount you can recover from the insurance company."

"It might take a lawsuit."

"Well, I'll give you one half of whatever I get out of it after we make arrangements with the lawyer."

"That might be too much."

"That'll suit me if it suits you."

"I'll see what can be done."

"And," she said, "I'll pay you regular wages to prove that my husband didn't steal those stones and didn't commit suicide. If he stole them, where are they now? It's absurd."

"No one else had the combination to the safe?"

"Not so far as we *know*; but someone must have. That's a fine safe. It couldn't have been opened without a combination. Look here, there's one thing I want understood. I don't want you to turn up any scandal in connection with

51

my dead husband."

"If I start digging up evidence, I can't tell what I'm going to find. I'll have to go right ahead digging it up."

"You wouldn't need to report everything you found, would you?"

"No."

"Well, go right ahead and dig."

"You think there's something you'd prefer not to have reported to you?"

She said, "Hilton was a good husband, kind, gentle, and considerate. I suppose, though, he wasn't any better than most men. If you ask me, you can't trust any of them."

She favored me with an arch smile.

"I'll start looking around," I said.

"And Nadine wants to see you."

"Where is she?"

"You'll find her in the nursery with Selma."

"Okay, I'll go look her up."

"And you'll really go to work on this, Mr. Lam?"

"I'll try."

"That's fine."

"By the way, how about the safe? Have you had it opened—since your husband's death?"

"Yes. We found some cryptic figures in his notebook. My lawyer suggested we send for a safe man to help us out. The safe expert worked out the combination to the safe from that list of figures that was in the notebook."

"Then you've gone through it—the safe?"

"Oh, yes."

"What was in it?"

"Just the insurance policies and a notebook in which Hilton had kept a complete record of his own case from the time it had first developed. Poor man, he thought he could at least keep some data that would be of benefit to the profession. I don't think it was really very serious— that is, I think he could have—well, if he'd taken care of

52

himself and hadn't kept driving himself day and night, he could have fought it off. Held it in check, you know. It might have been years and years before it got bad enough to take him off."

"I see."

She said, "My lawyer has fixed up an agreement with the insurance company by which they pay the forty thousand. There isn't any prejudice against our side of the case because we accept it. We can go ahead and try to collect the rest any time."

"Okay."

"And you won't forget to see Nadine?"

"I'm on my way."

She smiled at me and said, "I don't know what it is about you, Mr. Lam, that inspires me with such a feeling of confidence."

"Thank you."

I found Nadine Croy in the nursery. It was the first time I'd seen Selma. She had her mother's eyes, an easy, good-natured smile that brought dimples into both cheeks.

Mrs. Croy said, "This is Mr. Lam, sweetheart."

Selma toddled across the room to give me her hand. "How do you do," she said, speaking slowly, distinctly, and with each word accented precisely.

"Very well, thank you, and how are you?"

"I'm nice. Mamma says if I'm a good girl, she'll run the motion-picture machine tonight."

Mrs. Croy laughed. "I'm afraid I'm making her very vain," she said. "I took a lot of family pictures. She loves to see them over and over."

Selma looked at me seriously and said, in her childish voice, "Pictures of Uncle Doctor, too. Uncle Doctor's gone to sleep, and he isn't going to wake up any more at all."

"Is that so?"

She nodded with slow solemnity.

Mrs. Croy said, "I'll get Jeannette to take care of Selma.

I want to go where we can talk."

She pressed a button, and after a few moments, when the maid came to the door, said, "Will you stay with Selma, please, Jeannette?"

Jeannette gave me a smile of recognition, said, "Yes, Mrs. Croy," and held out her hands to Selma.

As I left the room, I felt that Jeannette was watching me with some interest. I noticed a mirror, placed at just the right angle so I could watch her reflection. She had crouched and was holding one arm around the child's waist. Her eyes were staring steadily at me. It was several seconds before she realized I was looking at her in the mirror, then she shifted her eyes and caught mine. For a moment only, she was startled. Then her lips parted to show even, white teeth as she smiled.

"This way," Nadine Croy said.

She took me out into the patio over to a secluded corner behind the big olla and the green vine. She indicated a couple of chairs which looked as though they had been placed there especially for the interview.

As soon as we were seated, she began abruptly, "Did Dr. Devarest tell you anything about me?"

"No."

"About—about my domestic problems?"

"No."

"You're certain?"

"Yes."

She waited as though trying to find the most advantageous angle of approach, then, apparently deciding to plunge right in, said, "My marriage was very unfortunate. I was divorced eighteen months ago. I had plenty of evidence I could have used against my husband, but I didn't want to. I only introduced enough evidence to get the decree—and, of course, the custody of Selma."

"Alimony?" I asked.

"No. I didn't need any. You see, that's the trouble. I

inherited rather a large sum of money from my father. Walter—Walter Croy, my husband—met me shortly after my father died. He was very kind, considerate, and helpful, and—well, I was attracted to him and married him.

"Shortly after the marriage, I realized that he was not at all insensible to the advantages of the money I had inherited. Then he began trying various schemes to get control of that money. Fortunately, because the estate was so large, it had been necessary to keep it in probate for some time, and I had an attorney who was very shrewd and very loyal. He warned me specifically against turning over the control of my property to my husband."

"Who's the lawyer?"

"Forrest Timkan."

"Then what happened?"

"I think Walter knew that Timkan had warned me against him. I don't know for certain, of course. As I made one excuse after another, Walter became more and more insistent, and then was when it became so plainly evident that the money was—well, really *all* he wanted."

"He didn't love you, you mean?"

She snapped her fingers and said, "He didn't care that much for me, or for any other woman. He's an exploiter. He's handsome, magnetic, and he twists women around his fingers. One woman means nothing whatever to him. That's what I'm getting at. After he found out that I'd been warned against turning over my property to him, he simply lost interest in everything. Not even Selma could hold him. He forged my name to checks, did half a dozen utterly despicable things. Well, as I say, I got my divorce, and, of course, custody of Selma."

"Then what happened?"

"About six months ago," she said, "Walter started attacking the problem from a new angle. He wanted part-time custody of Selma."

"I thought you said he didn't care much about her."

"He doesn't care a thing about her, but some day Selma is going to have money. That's something Walter would naturally take into consideration, and he also thought that—well, he put it up to me rather crudely."

"Put what up to you?"

"That I could buy him off."

"Did you do so?"

"No. Mr. Timkan said that once I started that, there'd be no end to it."

"So what happened?"

She said, "Walter was being really disagreeable. Then suddenly everything stopped." She looked at me with searching eyes. "Did Dr. Devarest tell you anything about that?"

"No."

"Well, everything was suddenly hushed up. Mr. Timkan couldn't understand it. But we were, of course, willing to let things ride along—let sleeping dogs lie.

"Yesterday," she went on, "Walter's lawyer rang up Mr. Timkan, said that there'd been a slight delay in connection with the presentation of the matter because Walter hadn't kept his word on bringing in money to cover fees and costs, but now the lawyer was ready to proceed."

"Why are you telling me this?" I asked.

"Because I think Dr. Devarest's death had something to do with all this. I've talked with Mr. Timkan about you, and he'd like to see you."

"All right, where do I find him?"

She took from a pocket of her blouse one of Timkan's cards, handed it to me. I looked at it, then dropped it in my pocket, and said, "All right, I'll go see him."

"I wish you'd feel free to—" She broke off and stood watching the man who had emerged from the living-room door to stand in the patio, looking at the fountain. He had bowed rather formally, but was obviously waiting for us to finish our conversation. I could see a puzzled, somewhat apprehensive expression on her face.

"Who is that?" I asked.

She said, "Corbin Harmley. One of the people Dr. Devarest befriended. He's been in South America on an oil proposition. He got in by air the day before Dr. Devarest died. He intended to come and see him the first thing, to pay back a loan."

"How much of a loan?"

"Two hundred and fifty dollars. It seems that he was very friendly with my uncle. He'd meet him at a luncheon club, and they'd chat. Harmley is a wanderer, a man who makes his living promoting oil leases and things, and he'd come and go, which is the reason Aunt Colette had never met him. Then he got badly down on his luck, and at just that moment had an opportunity to go to South America. My uncle staked him to the money he needed for expenses.

"Well, as I get the story, Harmley had a little good luck and a lot of bad luck for a while, and then he got hold of something that he thought would really work out. But it was a difficult matter, trying to handle it so the big corporations that wanted to get control wouldn't freeze him out. You know how they work."

"Go ahead."

"That's all there is to it. He's finally managed to get his deal all lined up and is putting it across. He flew back to the States in connection with this business matter, and one of the first persons he wanted to see was Dr. Devarest so he could pay back the loan and tell him the good news. Then he picked up a newspaper and read of his death. It was a terrible shock.

"He wrote Aunt Colette. It was a very fine letter. She showed it to me, one of the nicest letters I've ever read. He told her that at her convenience he'd like to call and make repayment of his loan.

"He told her some things about Dr. Devarest in the letter, things we'd never known—about how he had helped other people quietly, and unassumingly, not only with cash loans, but by encouraging them and backing them in every way."

"Then he came out to see your aunt?"

"Yes. She met him at the funeral. He asked if he might be permitted to attend, and—well, he certainly *is* nice, tactful, considerate. It seems at one time he'd started drinking pretty heavily, and Dr. Devarest straightened him out, gave him a stake to carry on."

"Why are you afraid of him?"

"I'm not—only—I think I've seen him before."

"Perhaps if you'd talk more frankly, I could listen more intelligently."

She laughed. "I'm really not beating around the bush," she said. "It's just that I don't know, and I don't want to get you off on the wrong trail. I've seen this man before. I'm almost certain that he came to the house one night to see my husband, Walter. I had only a brief glimpse of him. It was shortly after we'd been married."

"Have you asked him about it?"

"No, I haven't. I didn't feel like discussing my domestic affairs with him, and it may just be a case of mistaken identity."

I said, "Why are you telling me all this?"

"Because," she said, "in addition to what you're doing for Aunt Colette, I want you to help me. I want you to go see Mr. Timkan. I want you to find out, if you can, whether Mr. Harmley knows Walter. I can't get the idea out of my mind that Harmley may inadvertently have given my uncle some tip about Walter which enabled him to bring pressure to bear. I'm almost certain there was something, and whatever it is, we've *got* to find out about it."

"Are you afraid to go into court on the custody matter?"

Her eyes met mine for a moment, then shifted uneasily. She said evasively, "Selma is getting old enough to understand now. The testimony—well, it wouldn't do the child any good, and if Walter should ever get even a part-time custody, it would be terrible—for her, I mean."

I thought things over, then said, "I'll go see Timkan."

"Please don't spare any expense," she said. "This is something that is so important. Of course, I don't want you to throw money away, but—"

"I understand."

"Would you like to meet Mr. Harmley now?"

"Why not?"

She arose at once. We crossed the patio. Harmley watched us coming toward him. He was an interesting figure, a man in the middle thirties with an abundance of dark hair that swept back from a high forehead. He held his chin high, as though he had a lot of pride in himself and his work. His eyes were keen, penetrating, and held a touch of humor.

Mrs. Croy said, in a swift undertone, "I'm going to introduce you as a friend of the family. And from now on, we'll call each other by our first names. Aunt Colette thinks that's the way to handle it and—"

"Fine," I interrupted.

She performed the introductions. Harmley's hand clasped mine in a warm, firm grip. His voice when he spoke was low, but so well modulated that it gave one the impression of a dynamic reserve power.

"If," he said, "you were intimately acquainted with Dr. Devarest, you had the privilege of knowing a very remarkable man."

"I certainly thought so," I agreed.

"That man changed my entire life," he observed simply, started to say something else, then stopped, giving the impression that a feeling of gratitude was battling with a certain natural disinclination to talk about himself in connection with any tribute he wished to pay to Dr. Devarest.

Mrs. Croy said, "Well, I'm going to run along and see

how my child's getting on. You'll go see that person I mentioned, won't you, Donald?"

"I'll be glad to."

She smiled, moved away. Harmley, watching her speculatively, said, "You know, Lam, it's damn funny, but I have the distinct feeling that I've met that woman before somewhere, and for the life of me I can't place her. I can't remember where I've seen her." He swung his eyes back to mine. "I *know* I've seen her."

I said, "That frequently happens. I've felt the same way myself on several occasions."

"What is it? Do you suppose we've met people about whom we feel that way, and forgotten them, or—"

"More likely," I said, "you've sat across from her in a streetcar, happened to be attracted by her unusually large eyes, and now that you've met her have a vague recollection of having seen her before. Or perhaps sometime when you and Dr. Devarest came out of a restaurant, she was waiting in his car."

"By George, that must be it. But it certainly is a peculiar feeling."

"She has a cute little girl."

"Hasn't she? She and her husband are separated?"

"Divorced, I understand."

"Too bad."

"I understand you saw quite a bit of Dr. Devarest?"

"At intervals. I'd see him very frequently for a week or two, or perhaps a month or two at a time, and then wouldn't see him again for months."

"Did you and Dr. Devarest have many friendships in common?"

"Oh, yes. We were members of the same luncheon club. I gave up my regular membership some time ago, but I'd usually attend as Dr. Devarest's guest when I was in town. I haven't been here for some time. This last trip kept me away six or eight months."

60

I said, "Rather an interesting coincidence. About six or eight months ago, some man gave Dr. Devarest a tip on a certain person who was a mutual acquaintance—something that impressed Dr. Devarest very deeply at the time."

He looked at me searchingly. "I say, old chap, that's a bit vague, isn't it?"

"Yes."

He laughed. "I didn't mean to criticize, but—"

"I understand, but it's something his wife has been trying to find out about."

"You don't know who this chap was?"

"No."

"You don't know who the person under discussion might have been?"

"No."

He shook his head, frowned, and said, "I don't get it."

I said, "Well, I'm just asking questions here and there of a few of Dr. Devarest's acquaintances. You saw him six or eight months ago?"

He frowned thoughtfully. "About seven months ago to be exact."

"Did you see quite a bit of him at that time?"

"No. As it happens, I didn't. I only saw him for a very brief visit. We had lunch together two days in succession, and he met me after dinner at his office. One evening we chatted for some little time. He was telling me about the way he'd fixed up his study." Harmley stopped talking abruptly, and his eyes regarded me searchingly. He said, "Did Dr. Devarest take you into his confidence concerning his study?"

"The obsolete medical equipment?" I asked.

"Which housed the liquor and the detective stories," he supplemented, laughing.

I nodded.

"Hilton kept that pretty much a secret, I fancy," he said. "I guess only a few of his more intimate friends knew about it."

"Do you remember whether he mentioned having installed a safe when you talked with him?" I asked.

Harmley stared steadily at the fountain for quite a few seconds, before he said, "There was something about a safe—something said about a safe. Wait a minute. I think it was the second day I had lunch with him. He told me that he had just placed an order for one of the best wall safes money could buy. Seems to me he placed the order that day."

"Look here, Harmley, I'm going to be frank with you. It's rather important that we know what you and Dr. Devarest talked about just prior to that time."

"Why? Good heavens, do you think *I* gave him some information which was valuable to him?"

"Yes."

Harmley frowned. "I can't think of a thing I could have said."

"Try to recall any persons whom you discussed with Dr. Devarest at that time, and particularly what you said about them. Take a little time to think it over."

"That's something of a job," he said, "but I can do it if you want me to."

"I'd like very much to have you."

"Tell you what I'll do. I'll sit down this evening and try and reconstruct all of the conversation. I'll make a few notes as I go along, and then sometime within the next day or two, I'll talk to you about it. I hope I won't be boring you with a lot of foolish comments, but I'm afraid that will be about the size of it. You know how it is when you get together with someone you know and like after an absence. You ask what's become of this fellow or that fellow, and—"

"This may have been about someone that—look here, did you happen to show Dr. Devarest any photographs of people—perhaps some group photos of those who were associated with you?"

He said, "Why, yes. I was just starting on this South American thing, and I'd had my picture taken with a couple of chaps from South America, also with some of the landholders, and—and there was a picture I'd had taken in San Francisco. We were laughing about it, a picture I'd had taken at an amusement park. Now, that you speak of it, I remember Dr. Devarest wanted a copy of the picture. I gave it to him. What made you think of photographs, Lam?"

"I didn't think of them. I was asking questions."

"Well, you asked about photographs."

"Because they were a possibility."

He said, "Well, the photographs I showed Hilton couldn't have had any bearing on anything *you* were investigating. They showed a group that was interested in the South American properties, and Hilton was interested in the photograph merely because that South American venture meant so much to me."

"Dr. Devarest didn't have any money in it?" I asked casually.

He glanced at me quickly, said, "No—I wish that he had had now. You cover a hell of a lot of territory—with your questions."

"I try to," I said.

He didn't thaw out after that, but said with a rather frigid dignity, "I'm glad I met you, Mr.—Lam. I'll see you again perhaps."

I countered his formality with the breezy manner of a visiting delegate at a convention. "Oh, I'll be seeing you. I'm around here quite often."

He walked away, and a few moments later Nadine Croy came out from the place where she had been watching.

"Learn anything?" she asked.

"Not much. He gave Dr. Devarest a couple of photographs, group pictures showing some of the people who were associated with him in his South American venture."

"I don't see how that could have any bearing on the case."

"Neither did he. He thinks he's met you somewhere before."

"Then he *was* the man who came out to see Walter. Did you tell him—I mean, remind him?"

"No."

"Why not?"

"I thought it would be better to let him place you by himself. My business is to get information—not to give it."

"I can probably break the ice by telling him his face is familiar and—"

"No. Better let it ride along the way it is now."

"You didn't offend him, did you, Mr.—er—Donald?"

"Uh huh."

"How?"

"I asked him if Dr. Devarest hadn't had some money invested in the oil properties."

"Why did he mind that?"

"Because if that had been the case, Harmley would have been holding out on Mrs. Devarest."

"I don't understand."

"Suppose Dr. Devarest gave him two hundred and fifty dollars to put in the business. Suppose the business had suddenly become enormously profitable. He comes in and pays the two hundred and fifty dollars back as a loan."

"Wouldn't there have been some record, some—"

"There might not have been."

She thought things over, then looked at me with a half frightened expression in her eyes. "You don't trust people very much, do you, Donald?"

"No," I said. "Could you get your husband up to your lawyer's office?"

"Only if he thought he was going to get something."

I said, "Bring Harmley and your former husband together where someone who's trained to appreciate the significance of casual remarks can hear what they say as soon as they recognize each other."

"You mean Mr. Timkan?"

"If he's a good lawyer, he should be able to get a pretty good clue from what they say when they meet each other."

"I'll try to arrange it. I think it would be well to let everyone think you're—well, a particular friend of mine—act that way."

"Okay. I'll be devoted when Harmley is around."

"Only when someone is around."

"That's right. Who's the man going into the house?"

"Rufus Bayley, the chauffeur."

It was the same man I'd seen looking in through the tool house door the night Dr. Devarest died.

I said, "I'd like to look him over."

"Rufus," she called in a low, musical voice.

He was just opening the door. He whirled and his face changed expression. Then he saw me, and his face became a mask again. It was a big-featured face, one that gave an impression of good-natured power, like that of a Saint Bernard or a Great Dane.

"Yes, Mrs. Croy."

"Did you grease and oil my car yesterday?"

"Yes, Mrs. Croy."

"That enough?" she asked me in a low voice.

I saw the nephew, Jim Timley, leaving the house. "It's enough for right now," I said, and she dismissed him with a smile and a gesture.

Jim Timley came marching toward us across the patio. He moved with the nervous bustle of a man who believes in direct action. His sun-bleached eyes fastened on mine. "I've just been talking with Aunt Colette. She told me about you—about this friend-of-the-family business."

I nodded.

Timley said, "It puts Aunt Colette in a funny position."

"What does?"

"The friend-of-the-family idea."

"Go ahead."

"Dr. Devarest's friends have never heard him speak of you. Aunt Colette felt it might give people the wrong impression—you showing up that way right after Dr. Devarest's death, and apparently being one of the inner circle. So she thought it would be a better plan for you to be Nadine's particular friend."

"Mrs. Croy's already broken the news," I said. "I just want to get my signals straight. I'd hate to start running toward the wrong goal post."

"Or run out of bounds," Nadine Croy said. Her eyes were smiling at me now.

"How about passes?" I asked.

"Laterals strictly. On all forward passes, be sure your receivers are eligible."

"Thanks," I told her. "I will."

chapter 7

ELSIE BRAND SAID, "No, Donald, she hasn't been in all day —hasn't even telephoned."

I sat down and offered her a cigarette.

She shook her head. "Bertha doesn't like me to smoke during office hours."

I said, "Go ahead. I'm a partner now."

"So I understand."

She hesitated a moment, then took the cigarette and lit up.

We smoked for a while in silence. "I think it would be a good plan to raise your wages," I told her.

"Why?"

"Because you're always pounding away on the typewriter."

"Bertha would run a blood pressure of two hundred and ninety-five. I asked her for a raise last month, and she turned me down so hard I bounced."

"How much did you want?"

"Ten dollars more."

"You've got it," I said.

"You can't do that."

"Why?"

"I mean you can't make it stick."

"I think I can. You're raised. How about that smashed bicycle? Heard anything yet?"

"Not yet. I rang up the Auto Club this morning. I guess she was too smart for us on that one."

"Give them a ring again," I said, "just in case."

Elsie balanced her cigarette on the edge of the ash tray, dialed a number, asked for a name, and then after a moment said, "Miss Brand. Anything on that smashed bicycle yet?"

I saw the expression change on her face. She picked up a pencil and said, "Just a moment. . . . Nollie Starr, 681 East Bendon Street. . . . How much does she want? . . . Yes, it was my fault, I guess. I'm sorry. . . . Thank you very much."

She hung up the receiver and tore the page out of her notebook. "There you are," she said. "Her correct address. She'd waited to make a claim until after she'd had the bicycle repaired. The Auto Club has the bill for repairs. It's made out directly to her at that address."

I folded the paper, put it in my pocket, and said, "Better follow up on it and make sure the Auto Club has sent a check. I wouldn't want to have Miss Starr trace your license number and start making inquiries to find out where you work. She might change her living-quarters."

"Okay, I'll give them a ring tomorrow. I—"

The door pushed open, and Bertha Cool came striding into the office.

Elsie dropped the cigarette into the ash tray, ground out the end, swung back toward the keyboard of her typewriter. Bertha Cool made a half-turn to glare at us. I beat her to the punch. "Where have *you* been all day?" I asked.

Bertha's hard little eyes glittered triumphantly. "Fishing," she announced. "A perfectly swell day fishing, and don't try to make anything of it. I told you I was going to take life easy. Now, don't let me interfere with *your* little tête-à-tête. I know, Donald, that you're a full-fledged partner in the business. You'll remind me of it directly. But Elsie works here on a salary. So far, she hasn't considered herself sufficiently indispensable to demand a full partnership."

"Elsie and I were talking business."

"Indeed."

I nodded.

She started to say something, then caught herself, and, with some of the belligerency fading from her eyes, said, "Oh, about that bicycle?"

"Partially that."

"What else?"

I said, "Elsie was telling me that, with costs of living going up, she finds it increasingly hard to make both ends meet."

"Well, she was wasting her time trying to get sympathy out of you," Bertha said, her eyes hard and brittle once more. "She told her troubles to me last month, and—"

"She didn't get any sympathy from me either," I said. Mad as she was, Bertha showed surprise.

"She got cash," I said, "a ten-dollar raise."

Bertha had started to say something. The significance of my remark dawned on her just as she had her mouth open. She threw her mind into reverse. For a second, she stood with her mouth open, then the torrent of words came. "Why, you little squirt! *I'm* running this office! You may be a partner, but you can't raise salaries without *my* consent. And as far as that's concerned, you—"

I said to Bertha, "Wouldn't it be better to have our

quarrels in the private office?"

She stood looking at me, blinking her eyes rapidly. Abruptly she strode toward the private office. I followed her in, and kicked the door shut.

She was making a desperate effort to keep her self-control. She said, "I should have known it would be like this. That girl's no more entitled to a ten-dollar raise than she's entitled to a chauffeur-to drive her back and forth to work. She's getting paid at the same rate other stenographers in this line of work are paid. She's—"

"She's doing about twice as much work as any other stenographer I've ever seen."

"Well, what of it?" Bertha demanded. "She wanted the job. I hired her. There were a dozen others who wanted the job. Naturally, I picked the one who could do the most work. That's good business."

I said, "Times were tough then. Jobs were scarce. You could pick and choose. You can't do it any more."

Bertha jerked open the drawer of her desk, took out a long, ivory cigarette holder, jammed a cigarette into it so hard she doubled over the paper and broke the cylinder. She started to throw the cigarette away, then changed her mind, tore off the broken end instead, and pushed the rest of it carefully into the cigarette holder. She said, "You may not realize it, but I can dissolve this partnership at any time."

I said, "So can I."

"You!" she said. "You came here without a nickel in your pockets, and were hungry to boot. You dissolve a partnership that's giving you more money than you ever had before in your life! Don't make me laugh!"

I said, "And Elsie Brand gets her ten-dollar raise, or the partnership is dissolved."

Bertha's hand shook as she held the flame to the cigarette. She got up from the desk and walked over to stand at the window, her back turned toward me. After about a minute and a half, she turned back to face me. Her face was a mask. She said sweetly, "All right, lover, I can stand it if you can. Only remember, *you* don't get a salary any more. You draw half of the net proceeds, after paying expenses. The trouble with you is, you still think you're being generous with *my* money. That ten-dollar raise is just five dollars a month out of *your* pocket. What's new in the Devarest case?"

"I'm to see Nadine Croy's lawyer, a man by the name of Timkan. Do you know him?"

"No, never heard of him. What are you going to see him about?"

"The general situation."

"When?"

"Tomorrow morning. She's going to have a man there who she thinks has something on her former husband."

"What?"

"She thinks this man, Harmley, gave Dr. Devarest some bit of information which enabled him to put the screws on her husband. Whatever the proof was that Dr. Devarest had, it was probably in his safe and was stolen."

"When the jewels were taken?"

"Before that. He conceived the stolen-jewel idea so as to have something on which he could call in the police."

"Where are the jewels now?"

"I don't know. One ring was in the glove compartment, and—"

"Yes, I know that. But if Dr. Devarest took that jewelry, where is it—the rest of it, I mean?"

"I haven't found out yet."

"She should pay us a reward for that."

"Who?"

"Mrs. Devarest."

"For what?"

"For recovering her jewels."

"I haven't recovered them yet."

"You will."

"I'm not even certain Mrs. Devarest hired me to get the jewels back."

"What *did* she hire you for then?"

"To be a red herring."

"On what?"

"To keep Walter Croy from finding out the name of the person with whom his former wife was in love."

"What makes you think that?"

"Because they started in telling me I was to pose, not as a detective, but as an intimate friend of the family. Then they made it more specific. I was to be Nadine Croy's personal property."

"Well, what's wrong with that?"

"Nothing as far as I'm concerned. She's easy on the eyes, but she's a little too anxious to have it understood I'm her heart throb."

Bertha said, "I don't get it."

I said, "Walter Croy started in asking for custody of the child, trying to show that the mother wasn't a fit person to have the custody. Apparently he wasn't doing it because he cared anything about the child. He wanted money. Something happened, and he dropped the case like a hot potato. Then something else happened, and he picked it up again. The fact that he dropped it made Mrs. Croy think she was absolutely safe. She could do anything she wanted to. She might have become a little careless. Now, the matter is right back where it was seven months ago."

"How would it help her any to push you out in front as a boy friend?"

"They couldn't prove any indiscretions with me, and it would keep the interested parties from looking any further."

Bertha Cool's eyes narrowed. "You *may* have something there."

"I'll know pretty soon," I said.

"How?"

"If she starts dragging me around in public with her, it'll mean I'm right."

"Why all the hooey? After all, she's divorced now."

"When I find that out, I'll know a lot more about what she's afraid of."

"You think she's afraid?"

"Of course."

The telephone rang.

Bertha picked up the receiver and said, "Who is it, Elsie?" Then she turned to me and said, "That Croy woman is on the line. Elsie told her you were in conference and couldn't be disturbed. She wants to know if you're free tonight. She says her Aunt Colette thinks it would be a good plan if you were seen together in public."

"Tell Elsie I'll call back in half an hour."

Bertha transmitted the message and slammed up the receiver with sufficient violence to threaten to smash the telephone. "She's falling for you."

I said, "That's nice. She's got a few hundred thousand in her own name. I might marry her and retire."

Bertha said grimly, "Suppose her intentions aren't honorable?"

I got up and started for the door. "To the pure," I announced, "all things are pure."

Six hundred and eighty-one East Bendon Street was a brick-sided, ornate-faced apartment house with a lot of gingerbread decorations over the door; a drab lobby with the usual assortment of faded, worn furniture. To one side was a door marked *Manager*, two steps and a hallway, with apartments on each side. There were three stories in the building and no elevator. Apartment 304 was on the third floor near the front of the house. The name on the mailbox showed it was held by Dorothy Grail. I rang the doorbell. There were sounds of motion. The door opened a three-inch crack—to the limit of a safety chain which stretched taut across the opening. A pair of intense black eyes regarded me curiously.

I said, "Does Miss Starr live here?"

"No. This is Miss Grail's apartment."

"And there isn't a Miss Starr living here?"

"No."

"You know a Miss Starr?"

"No." The door started to close.

I kept my voice low, talked with quick, jerky sentences. "I can't understand that. I'm from the Auto Club. She gave this address. I'm to make an adjustment on her bicycle."

I heard the sound of quick, light footfalls, and Nollie Starr's voice saying, "That's different, Dot. Let him in."

The black-eyed girl slipped the safety catch. I entered the apartment. It was a two-room affair, a dinky little kitchen, and a combined living-room and bedroom with a big wall bed.

It took Nollie Starr just a moment to place me. First, the realization that my face was familiar, then anger and fear in her eyes.

A man was sitting over in a chair by the table in the corner of the room. He looked up as he heard Nollie Starr take that quick, startled inhalation of breath. The light shone full on his face. It was Jim Timley.

I said, "Good evening. I don't want to interrupt a tête-à-tête, but I thought this might be a good time to get acquainted."

Timley pulled his feet in under him, but it was his arms that raised him out of the chair more than his legs. He looked as limp as a piece of cooked asparagus.

The black-eyed girl seemed to be the only one who didn't want to run. She regarded me curiously, not getting the play.

73

I said, "My name's Lam. I guess no one's going to introduce us. You're Dorothy Grail. Now we all know each other. Do we talk here, or would you two prefer to leave Dorothy out of it?"

Dorothy Grail pushed the door shut, turned the bolt, and said, "Why not talk here?"

Timley said, "Look here, Lam. I can explain this—but I don't know as I'm called on to do so." He looked at Nollie Starr, got a little more courage, and said, "Frankly, I don't see that it's any of your damn business."

Nollie Starr nodded approvingly.

Timley liked the approach. The more he saw of it, the more sold he got on it. He came barging toward me, his shoulders squared; the lean, bronzed face twitched slightly with nervous emotion. I could see from the swing of his shoulders he added boxing to his other athletic accomplishments.

"I never did care for snoops, and I don't like you. You came in that door. You've got until I count three to get out of it. One—two—"

I said, "None of it is *my* business. I'm simply hired to present facts to Mrs. Devarest. I'll report to her, and you can explain to her."

Timley's voice held sudden panic. "Come back here."

I said, "If you've got any other ideas, start talking."

Timley looked at the girl. He looked as helpless and frightened as a kitten on top of a telegraph pole.

Nollie Starr said smoothly, "Since you've interfered so frequently in my private affairs, I may as well tell you the answer."

"It'll save time," I said.

Nollie Starr spoke with the smooth, easy assurance of a woman in perfect command of the situation. "You certainly *do* jump at conclusions, Mr. Lam," she said and laughed.

"Go ahead," I told her. "Think fast."

Her eyes showed indignation. "You listen to me," she said. "I don't have to think fast. I'm tired of having you dogging me around. Now then, just to show you where you get off, I'll tell you a little secret. I live here. I've been living here for six months. This is my roommate, Dorothy Grail. Because we had a lease on the apartment, I kept up my end, and I wasn't certain how permanent my job was going to be out at Dr. Devarest's. A couple of months ago when it was raining, Jim Timley took me home. He met Dorothy. Since then, he's been coming back occasionally. Usually, I try to give them a break and get out when he calls, unless he's taking Dot somewhere. Tonight I didn't want to do it because I hadn't made up my mind just what to do about this other matter.

"I'll admit I made a mistake in running out when Dr. Devarest told me to call the police. I had a reason for doing so. I'm not going to tell you what that reason was. I'm not going to tell anyone what it was. If I keep out of sight until the authorities find whoever stole the jewels, I won't have to tell anyone anything.

"Jim Timley understands the entire situation. He can vouch for me."

"That's right," Timley said hastily. "She's telling you the truth, Lam."

Nollie Starr went on with that same rapid vehemence. "All I want is to be left alone. I'm minding my own business, and I want other people to mind theirs. And if you *really* want to do me a favor, you can quit tagging me around, and find out who really stole those jewels."

"Have you any ideas?" I asked.

She looked at Timley, hesitated, said, "I'm not sticking my chin out."

Timley looked at his watch, hesitated a moment, picked up his hat. "I want to talk with you, Lam," he said. "I'll walk as far as the corner. My car's in the parking lot."

Nollie Starr looked at him significantly for a moment,

75

vanished in the direction of the kitchenette. Dorothy Grail walked toward him and gave him her hand. "Good night, Jim," she said. "I'm sorry."

"It's all right."

"I know how you feel—how embarrassed you are over anything like this. I'm sorry it happened. It was nothing I could prevent. It wasn't my fault. You understand that, don't you?" There was anxiety in her voice.

"Of course," he said impatiently.

She clung to him. "Jim, you're not going to—it won't make any difference, will it?"

"No."

Her arm came around his neck. Her face was close to his. "Jim, dear—promise."

He seemed impatient to get free. "No," he said. "I tell you it won't make any difference."

"You *darling*," she said, and held half-parted lips up to his. He bent over and put a listless arm around her waist. He seemed preoccupied, anxious to get away.

I stood there, waiting for them to break up the clinch.

Timley's arm tightened. His other hand came up to the back of her neck. She twined her fingers in his hair. Their shoulders swayed slightly.

Nollie Starr, coming in from the kitchenette, called, "Time! Come up for air, you two."

It was Dorothy Grail who pushed herself free. Jim Timley's eyes were drinking her in. The lipstick formed a red smear on his lips. His face was flushed.

"You don't need to come on my account, Timley," I said.

He turned toward me. "That's all right. I—I want to talk with you." He turned back to Dorothy Grail. "You *bet* it isn't going to make any difference," he said.

There was laughter in her eyes. She glanced past him to Nollie Starr, then back to Timley. "Be your age, Jim," she said, "and run along with the nice detective and tell him everything he wants to know."

Timley picked up his hat.

Nollie Starr said, "Watch those lips, Timley. Dorothy leaves a wicked smear. And don't forget your books. We've enjoyed them a lot."

She came to stand in front of him, and, with a handkerchief wrapped around her index finger, wiped the lipstick off his face. She handed him a package wrapped and tied with cord.

Timley said, "Good night, Nollie," turned to Dorothy, looked at her, started to say something, changed his mind, and swung back toward me.

"Good night—sweetheart," Dorothy said.

He acted as though he wanted to kiss her again.

I said, "Well, I've got work to do," and opened the door.

Timley came hurrying after me. We walked down the steps together. At the sidewalk, he said, "Look here, Lam, you seem like a decent chap."

"Thanks."

"You look like the sort of man who would listen to reason."

"What sort of reason?"

He said, "I don't know whether it's ever occurred to you to consider my exact relationship in the Devarest household."

"If it hasn't, it will," I told him.

He said, "Aunt Colette is self-centered and vain. She happens to control every dollar I have or can ever hope to get. My folks left me penniless. Aunt Colette put me through college; then she wanted me to travel. I was willing. She wanted to go along. Well, that was all right, too. She liked to be squired around by a young man. After a while she quit telling people I was her nephew. The trip got pretty ghastly after that. I saw a good deal of the world, South America, the Orient, and Europe. I paid quite a price for it. Aunt Colette kept me with her almost constantly. However, there were times after she'd go to bed when I could sneak out for a few hours, and really see some of the places I wanted to see.

"We came back. She wanted me to stay on in the house with her for a few months. She thought I needed building up. I'd picked up a tropical dysentery, and it was bothering me. Dr. Devarest told me to take it easy for a while and to get plenty of sunlight and fresh air. Well, things started drifting. I sort of got in the habit of being there. Dr. Devarest liked to have young people around. I think Aunt Colette bored him to distraction."

Timley took a deep breath, turned to meet my eyes, and said, "That is the real low-down on the whole situation. It's a mess. Sometimes I feel like a heel, but I wasn't fitted for anything. I had an education along cultural lines. Don't think I've taken it lying down. I've gone out and tried to get jobs. I've gone to the airplane factories. They've promised to investigate and let me hear from them. What happens is they look me up, find that I'm living with relatives and am supposed to be something of a playboy. Of course, I have to keep from letting Aunt Colette know that I've been looking for work.

"Well, I suppose I'm a prize heel. I've decided to settle down to it. She's promised to remember me in her will. She says I'm still suffering from the effects of those tropical diseases, that I'm not strong enough to get out and really work, that when I've fully recovered, she'll be glad to help me get into something. She could do it, too, if she used her influence, or, rather, if she'd got Dr. Devarest to use his. But she'd never think I was fully recovered. It was always another few weeks of sunlight and fresh air."

"Your Aunt Colette will live a long time," I said.

He acted as though he wanted to say something, but didn't.

"Another twenty-five or thirty years of this, and you'll be quite the faded Beau Brummell," I said, goading him on to make him say the thing that was trembling on the end of his tongue.

It came out with a rush. "Aunt Colette won't live more than two or three years at the most. It's a heart condition that becomes progressively worse. Dr. Devarest knew of it, but never told her. He said she'd go suddenly when she went, and it was better to let her live her life the way she wanted, and then go all at once."

"Who told you about this? Dr. Devarest?"

He shook his head. "Nadine," he said. "Dr. Devarest told her, and she told me. Probably she shouldn't, but—well, she knew how I felt. I can't explain it exactly, Lam, but Aunt Colette has been frightfully jealous. Perhaps I shouldn't say that, but she doesn't like to have me take an interest in girls. She makes a lot of excuses, saying that women would interfere with regular hours, that I'd be running around at all hours of the night, that I should keep out in the open air, and have lots of sunlight. But the fact is, she's just plain jealous. She wants to be the center of attraction everywhere. She wants really to rule the roost. Oh, I'm not telling you anything that can't be verified. Ask Nadine sometime."

I said, "If Nadine Croy doesn't like it there, why the devil doesn't she get out? She's not financially dependent on—"

"If you can find the answer to that," Timley told me, "you're a better detective than I am."

"You mean your aunt has some hold on her?"

He shrugged his shoulders, said, "I'm talking too damn much."

"Not enough."

He said, "Look here, Lam, could we—could we reach some understanding?"

"No."

"You aren't going to tell Aunt Colette about Dorothy Grail?"

"I'm working for your aunt."

"But you're trying to recover the jewels, and prove that Dr. Devarest didn't deliberately commit suicide. You're trying to collect insurance. My affair with Dorothy—if you want to call it that—doesn't enter into it."

"I'll think it over," I told him. "Good night."

He stood on the curb, watching me walk away.

chapter 8

I DROVE ABOUT SIX BLOCKS, stopped in at a drugstore, called police headquarters, and asked for Lieutenant Lisman of the Jewel Theft Detail. He was on nights and had just come in.

"This is Lam talking," I said, "Donald Lam of the firm of Cool & Lam, Private Detectives."

His voice held no welcoming recognition. "Yeah. What do *you* want?"

"I want to give you a tip on those Devarest jewels, but I don't want you know where it came from."

There was interest in his voice now, but that was all. "What's the tip?"

I said, "Listen, we're working for Mrs. Devarest, trying to clear up certain angles of the case. If she knows I told you what I'm going to spill, she'll fire me. You'll have to protect me."

"You sound like it was something important."

"It is."

"Okay, what?"

"Is it a deal?"

"Yes."

"Nollie Starr," I said, "Mrs. Devarest's social secretary. She vanished about the same time the jewels did. You'll find her in an apartment at 681 East Bendon Street. The apartment's in the name of Dorothy Grail, her roommate. You'll have to work fast, because she may take a powder."

"You're Lam?" Lieutenant Lisman asked.

"That's right. Donald Lam."

"And that address is 681 East Bendon Street?"

"That's right."

"And the name the apartment is under is Gail?"

"No," I said. "Grail. G-r-a-i-l."

There was friendliness in Lisman's voice now. "I'll owe you one for this," he said, and then after a moment added cautiously, "if it works out."

"It'll work out," I said, and hung up.

I drove to the Devarest residence. There was a light in the chauffeur's room over the garage. I parked the car by the side entrance, walked noiselessly along the driveway, climbed the stairs, and knocked.

Rufus Bayley, the chauffeur, opened the door.

His appearance confirmed the previous impression I'd formed of big, good-natured power. But I wasn't certain that the good nature wasn't more or less a mask. His six feet of big-boned frame was loose-knit, easy-moving. His thick, black, curly hair was a tumble of confusion. He grinned, and the light caught a scar on his left cheek.

"I'm Donald Lam," I told him.

"Yeah, I know. What do you want?"

"I want to come in."

He stood to one side. "Come on."

The room had three outside walls with plenty of windows. There were Venetian blinds over the windows. The blinds looked new. The furniture was plain. The rugs were somewhat faded and worn thin. There was a bookcase fairly well filled with books. I moved over to get a quick glimpse of titles. They were the best sellers of six months ago. The room was neat and well cared for.

Bayley said, "Sit down."

I dropped into what looked like the most comfortable chair. He sat down across from me. His face still wore that good-natured grin. He said, "You don't need to pull that friend of the family stuff on me because Mrs. Devarest told me all about you. I'm to co-operate with you."

"That's fine."

"Anything you want to know?"

"Yes."

"I'll give you anything I can."

"How long you been here?"

"About six months."

"You came to work about the same time Nollie Starr did?"

The smile remained on his lips. His eyes quit smiling. "I think she was here when I came."

"But she hadn't been working very long?"

"No."

"Who takes care of the place up here?"

"I do."

"You keep it looking neat."

"I like it that way."

"There isn't any wall bed in this room?"

"No."

"Where do you sleep?"

He motioned toward the wall which held only a single door. "There's another room in there."

"I want to look at it."

I got up, and he got up. For a moment, he shuffled uneasily as though debating whether to walk across and open the door. I walked over toward the door with calm assurance. He cat-footed along behind me. "Whatcha looking for?" he asked. The good-natured note had left his voice. It had a sharp edge.

"Surveying the premises," I told him, and opened the door.

It was a large bedroom with three outside walls. There were windows in here, and Venetian blinds on the windows. There was a single white iron bed, and a big double bed of walnut, also a walnut dressing-table with a mirror and lights on each side of the mirror. There was a bureau of cheap, stained pine with a wavy mirror. There were several chairs, a few, thin, worn rugs and a fine Navajo rug by the side of the double bed. A bathroom was sandwiched in between the two rooms with a single window. I looked in the bathroom. It was neat and clean. The window ran almost the full width of the bathroom. There were Venetian blinds there, too.

"Nice quarters," I said.

"Uh huh."

"You like these Venetian blinds?"

"Yeah. They give you a lot of ventilation, and then when you want, you can let in the sunshine, too."

"You're a pretty good housekeeper."

"I aim to be. I like things kept up. I keep the cars in good shape, and keep the garage clean and tidy. I have a vacuum cleaner to use on the car cushions, and I bring it up here and go over things."

"You do quite a bit of reading?"

"Uh huh."

"You aren't kept very busy?"

"That's what *you* think." The good-natured grin was back on his face now.

"Do you drive for anyone except Mrs. Devarest?"

"Occasionally Mrs. Croy."

"She has her own car?"

"Yes."

"But you keep it up?"

"That's right."

"How about Timley? Does he have a car?"

"Yes."

"You keep that up?"

"Uh huh."

"And Dr. Devarest's car?"

"He never wanted his car kept up. He had it greased and serviced down at the garage in the Medical Building. I don't think he ever washed it. They'd wipe it off once in a while. It would stand out in the weather when he was making calls. He used to washboard a fender every once in a while and leave it that way, said the only use he had for a car was to call on patients."

I walked over to the bureau. A plain black hairbrush and comb were on it, a box of talcum powder, a bottle of hair tonic, and a bottle of shaving-lotion. There was a crystal-backed hairbrush and comb on the dressing-table.

"Where does that door lead?"

"The closet."

I opened the door. The closet was large. It, too, had a window—and more Venetian blinds. Several suits of clothes on hangers, four or five pairs of shoes, and an assortment of neckties on a tie rack. I noticed a silk scarf on the tie rack.

"You do all the housework—making your own bed, and all that?"

"Yes."

I looked at the neatly made beds. "Looks as though you'd fallen heir to some castoff bedroom furniture from the main house."

"That's right. Mrs. Devarest changed the bedrooms around, put in some other stuff, and sent the surplus out here."

Both beds were made up. I said, "You're given the privilege of having a guest occasionally?"

The grin was back on his face. "Occasionally."

I walked back to the sitting-room and sat down in the chair. "Want a cigarette?" I asked, holding my cigarette case toward him. He took one. We both lit up.

"Anything else you want to know?"

"Yes."

"What?"

"I first saw you looking through the door to the garage the night Dr. Devarest's body had been discovered."

"That's right."

"You didn't stay."

"Shucks, no. I saw the place crawling with police. You see, it was my night out. I came in to go to bed. The maid told me Dr. Devarest was dead. I looked in, saw the bulls and the coroner, and decided I couldn't help any. I hadn't been around when it happened, and so I ducked out of the garage."

"You stood in the door for a minute or two."

"Yes."

"Where did you go after that? You didn't come upstairs. If you did, I didn't hear you."

He said, "Those stairs are built pretty solid. I'm kinda light on my feet."

"Then you did come up here?"

"Yes."

"Right away?"

"Well, not exactly right away. A little later."

"It was some time later, wasn't it?"

"What's that got to do with it?"

"I want to know."

His eyes were sullen now, and the mouth was closed in thick-lipped defiance. He kept silent.

"How much later?" I asked.

"I can't tell you."

"Why not?"

"I didn't look at my watch."

"It might have been a half hour later?"

"Well—yes, it might have been."

"And it might have been several hours later?" I said.

"I tell you I don't see what this has to do with it."

I said, "At the time you left the place, as I remember it, the police were talking about taking fingerprints. They'd just found the jewel cases."

He said, "Now listen, buddy, you're probably a smart little runt. I don't know. You've got your racket, and I've got mine. I'm not interfering with you, and I don't want you to interfere with me. I wasn't here the whole evening. If necessary, I can prove where I was. I don't know a damn thing about those sparklers. Now lay off of me."

I said, "That's a nice scarf you have in the closet."

I saw a puzzled look come into his eyes. "Scarf?"

"Yes. That pink silk scarf."

"Oh."

"Is it yours?"

He hesitated a minute, then said, "No."

"Whose is it?"

He did a little thinking, then said, "I don't know as that's any of your business."

"It might be."

He laughed suddenly and said, "Forget it. Don't try pushing me around."

"I'm not pushing you around. I want to know whose scarf it is."

"I don't know whether it's Mrs. Devarest's or Mrs. Croy's. I found it in the car when I was cleaning up. I intended to ask about it. I took it upstairs, and then in the excitement of what happened, I clean forgot about it. I'll find out which one it belongs to. Now then, you know damn near everything about me."

"I suppose the rugs were in here when you moved in?"

"What's that got to do with it?"

"They were, weren't they?"

"Yes."

"That Navajo rug came in later?"

"Yes."

I nodded toward the windows. "Looks as though they'd had curtains on them at one time."

He didn't say anything.

"When were the Venetian blinds put in? About three months ago?"

"Something like that."

"Can you tell me exactly how long ago?"

He thought for a while, then said, "Four months."

I said, "Well now, let's see. You found that scarf when you were cleaning the car, intended to ask about it, and then the excitement incident to Dr. Devarest's death wiped it out of your mind."

He didn't answer that one, but after I kept waiting, nodded his head slowly.

"Then you must have found the scarf the day the jewels were stolen or the day after."

"The day after."

"That was the day Dr. Devarest died?"

"Yes."

"Did you have all day off or just the night?"

"Just the evening."

"When did you find the scarf, in the morning or afternoon?"

"What are you driving at?"

"If you'd found it in the morning," I explained, "you'd have asked questions about it. You'd hardly have brought it up here with you unless you'd found it about the time you quit work. You didn't want to take it into the house and ask questions then, because you probably had a date, and didn't want to be late."

He thought that over for a while, then said, "Well, yes."

"Therefore, you must have found it, say around five o'clock."

"Somewhere around there."

"Did you have dinner in the house that night?"

"Yes."

"You eat with the servants in the kitchen?"

"Yes."

I said, "Let's take a look at that scarf. It may be important."

"I don't see why."

"One of the women had the car out the day after the gems were stolen. You weren't acting as chauffeur on that trip, otherwise you'd have remembered which one had been wearing the scarf. You found the scarf and didn't know which of the two women it belonged to. Therefore, it must have been left in the car on a trip made probably late that afternoon. It was a trip you didn't know about. Otherwise, you'd have known which one of the women had been using the car and had the maid simply return it to whichever one it belonged. The fact that you didn't ask the maid about it indicates that you had an idea in the back of your mind whoever was driving the car didn't want the other woman to know she'd taken the trip. What was it? A date with someone?"

"You figure out a hell of a lot of stuff from nothing at all, don't you?"

"Not from nothing at all—from a scarf."

He said, "You're doing a lot of mind reading from it."

I said, "That's right. Why didn't you think the woman who owned the scarf would want the other woman to know she'd been using the car?"

"I tell you I didn't think any of that stuff out. I found it just before I knocked off. I carried it up here and forgot about it."

"You said the reason you forgot about making inquiries was the excitement over Dr. Devarest's death."

"That's right."

"You didn't work on the car after you'd had dinner Wednesday night. Dr. Devarest didn't die until late Wednesday."

He said, "You guessed it the first time, buddy. I had a date. I was cutting things pretty fine. I beat it right after dinner to keep this date. Now, does that explain it?"

I said, "Yes, there were three women: Mrs. Devarest, Mrs. Croy, and Nollie Starr. That couldn't have been Nollie Starr's scarf, could it?"

"No."

"Are you certain?"

"Well, not entirely."

I said, "Let's look at the scarf."

He didn't move right away, but, after a moment, got up out of the chair with that loose-jointed, graceful, easy motion, and walked into the bedroom. After he'd got started, I followed along behind. He went into the closet, and I moved over toward the dressing-table. My thumb and finger pinched into the hairbrush on the dressing table, and brought out several hairs. I twisted them around my forefinger, and pushed them down into my vest pocket. He came out of the closet with the scarf. I moved over and took it from his hands, and stood under the light, studying it. After a few moments, I handed it back to him.

"Nothing on it to indicate which woman it belongs to," he said, feeling me out. He shoved the scarf down into the side pocket of his coat.

I said, "It's Jeannette's—the maid's."

He couldn't keep the expression out of his face.

"It's hers," I said patiently.

"What makes you think so?"

"The color wouldn't have gone with Mrs. Devarest's complexion. It's of too cheap material to have been bought by Mrs. Croy. You yourself said Nollie Starr was out. That leaves Jeannette. Also the perfume on it is the same scent she uses."

"Trying to get my goat?" he asked angrily.

"No, just telling you facts."

I walked back to the sitting-room and sat down again. He went over to his chair, started to sit down, then changed his mind and stood there, waiting for me to go.

I ground out the stub of my cigarette. He looked at his watch. I said casually, "Did you get a raw deal—when they sent you up?"

"I'll say I did. I—" He stopped and stood staring at me. His face was twisted with anger. "Damn you," he said. "You and your snooping goddamed questions! You—"

"Never mind that," I told him. "I knew you'd been sent up the way you acted over those fingerprints. Sit down and tell me about it."

He walked completely around the chair before he sat down.

"What about it?"

He said, "All right, so what? I was sent up. It didn't amount to much."

"What was it for?"

"Check-kiting. Every time I'd get crocked, I'd go crazy. I'd give checks. They didn't amount to much; ten, fifteen, and twenty-five bucks. Usually there'd be about a hundred dollars' worth of them. After I'd get sober, the checks would begin to come in, and they'd bounce. I'd find out who had 'em and go around and square it."

"With money?"

"I didn't have any money."

"How did you square it?"

"Oh, various ways."

"You paid them back?"

"Sure. All of them. I made them good. The fellows would put the checks in the till, and I'd save up my wages until I had enough to cover them, or maybe I'd work 'em out—if I could."

"Without getting drunk in the meantime?"

He said, "I'd only go on a binge about once every four or five months. When I did, I made a damn good job of it. I'm like that."

"How about the time you were sent up?"

He said, "The checks bounced. The boss fired me for being crocked, and not showing up. It came out of a clear sky."

"He hadn't fired you on any of the other occasions?"

"No. He'd give me a talking to, and I'd promise to cut it out. This time things were just a little worse than before. I stayed away a little longer."

"How long?"

"About three days."

"What was your job?"

"Chauffeur."

"How long did you get?"

"A year."

"How long ago?"

"A couple of years. That cured me. I haven't been on a binge since, and I haven't given any rubber checks. I didn't like that year. Now, what are you going to do about it? You go in and spill that stuff to the boss, and I'm bounced out of a job. I won't get a letter of recommendation. I won't be able to get another job, and first thing you know, I'll be back where I started."

"Where did you do your stretch?"

He shook his head.

"That's out. I've put all the cards you have a right to see on the table."

"What do you stand to lose by telling me about where you did your stretch?"

He said, "I did that under my right name. I had to, because that was the moniker that was on the paper. The folks haven't heard about it. They aren't going to. My mother thinks I was in China. She's old. If she knew I'd been in stir, it would take her off. It don't make a damn bit of difference. That's why I didn't want the bulls taking my fingerprints. I took the name of Bayley after I got out. I never use my real name except when I'm writing letters to Mother, and I get those sent to me General Delivery."

I got up, and he followed me to the door. "You going to tell anybody about this?" he asked.

"Not right away."

"Ever?"

"I don't know."

He started to close the door. I turned on the step. "One more question."

"What?"

"When you're up here, can you hear a car running in the garage?"

"Not if the motor's idling. The way I keep those cars, it's darn hard to hear them, even if you're standing close to them. But I can usually hear it when they start a car down in the garage. That all?"

I said, "Yes." He slammed the door.

chapter 9

I WENT OVER to the house. Dr. Gelderfield had just left. Mrs. Devarest was "being brave." She was also very much wrapped up in herself and her symptoms.

"I simply mustn't let it get me down," she told me. "I must look at it from a calm, logical standpoint."

"That's right."

"Death is inevitable, you know, Donald—I'm going to start calling you Donald, too, because everyone else does."

"That's fine."

"And you may call me Colette."

"Thank you."

"Particularly when anyone's around. You know, you're supposed to be Nadine's friend, her—well, her very particular friend."

"I understand."

"You don't mind, do you?"

"No."

"Well, Dr. Gelderfield says there's only one thing for me to do, that I must get new interests. He says that death is inevitable, that time is the great healer of wounds. That's only another way of saying that new experiences wipe out the memories of the old."

"Sounds logical."

"Doesn't it? He says some women shut themselves up and mourn and don't get any new experiences, and it takes them years and years to get to the point where the wound heals. By that time, they may have done themselves some serious injury, mentally. They've got the habit of brooding and feeling sorry for themselves. He says the thing for *me* to do is to take a realistic view and plunge into a life of normal activities so I'll have new experiences to wipe out the terrible ache."

"You agree with him?"

"I don't *want* to, not the way I feel now, but, of course, it's a physician's prescription. Medicine isn't always agreeable to the taste, but if you have confidence in the doctor, you take it."

"That's right."

"I just don't know *what* to do. Doctors tell me that my trouble is all nervous, that I'm simply too high-strung, that my perceptions are delicate. You wouldn't think I was one of those nervous, jittery women. That's because I've lived a full, normal life. I haven't the nervousness that characterizes so many thin, emotionally starved women. I've really lived—but *you're* not interested in that," she said, looking at me archly with those pop eyes of hers. "You're a thinking, reasoning machine that's interested only in crime puzzles. Mrs. Cool told me that. But she said women went simply crazy over you. Tell me, Donald, have you found that to be the case, or was she simply trying to arouse my curiosity?"

I said, "You can't ever tell about Bertha. She may have been trying to arouse your curiosity."

"I guess perhaps it's your—it's a preoccupation. It's not a complete indifference to feminine charms. I'm sure of that."

"Maybe you're right."

"You seem to be thinking about your work all the time."

"In this business, you can't afford to go to sleep on the job."

"No, I suppose not. But some of the women who have hired you must have been lonely and frightened and wanted to—"

"They wanted me to do some particular job and get it over with."

"Of course, you can't expect a woman to come right out and *tell* you. You have to use a certain amount of subtlety."

"Perhaps that's it," I said. "I'm not subtle. What became of Dr. Devarest's notebook?"

"Why, I have it."

I said, "I'm trying to check up on the calls Dr. Devarest made that Wednesday night. I believe there were two calls which he finally decided he'd have to make. There were some patients with whom he talked over the telephone. You gave Dr. Devarest the list of patients who had called during the day. Isn't there some way by which we can tell which ones he called on, and which ones he handled over the telephone?"

"Would that have anything to do with the insurance?"

"I don't know. He may have had the missing jewelry in the glove compartment of the automobile ready to restore to you. After he died, someone took it out of the glove compartment."

"Is there anything—any evidence that makes it look as though he might have got the jewelry from someone after he left here?"

"Not that so much as evidence of something else."

"What?"

"One of the rings was still in the case. That would indicate someone had gone through the jewel cases either very hastily or very carelessly."

"Why should one be careless in dealing with valuable jewelry?"

"Because it had only been taken for a blind, and it was intended the jewelry should eventually be returned. Under those circumstances, a person might be careless."

"Donald, that's exactly the theory I told you to avoid. I want to prove that Hilton didn't have anything to do with taking that jewelry."

"I understand; but you asked me why anyone should be careless. That's it. But there's another theory."

"What is it?"

"That Dr. Devarest recovered the jewels from the thief. He drove into his garage, fully intending to return the jewelry to you. He had some repairs he wanted to make on the car first. He became overcome with monoxide fumes. Someone else came into the garage, found him lying there, and thought it might be possible to get the jewelry out of the glove compartment without being discovered."

"Donald, that's the theory I like."

"We'll work on it then."

"Do that."

"Very well."

"Then this person must have known the jewels were in the car?"

"That's right."

"Who could that person have been?"

"I don't know—yet."

"But you're working on it?"

"Yes."

"Then you'll get the jewels back?"

I said, "That's the smallest part of it."

"I don't think I understand."

I said, "The only key to the glove compartment was the ignition key in the car. The only way you could get the key out of the ignition was to shut the motor off and take the key out."

"Well?"

I said, "Therefore, any person who entered the garage and wanted to get the jewels out of the glove compartment would first have to shut off the motor on the car, turn the ignition lock, take the key out, and unlock the glove compartment."

"Yes, of course. You've explained that."

"But," I said, "the motor was running when we found Dr. Devarest's body."

"You mean, then, whoever did it put the key back in the ignition lock?"

"Yes, then unlocked the ignition, turned on the motor, and went away and left it running."

"Why?"

"To cover up the evidence of the crime—the fact that he'd taken the jewels."

"But doesn't that make the taking of the jewels the thing of the greatest importance?"

"No."

"I don't see what you're getting at."

I said, "If Dr. Devarest drove into the garage, left the motor running, started tinkering with the automobile, and became overcome by the fumes of carbon monoxide, without the interposition of some other act or agency over which he had no control, his death was accidental, but it wasn't a death by accidental *means*. He'd set in motion every one of the factors which brought about his death."

"That's what my lawyers have told me. I don't think it's just. I don't think—"

"But," I interrupted, "if someone shut off the motor *before* Dr. Devarest was dead, even if at that time he was lying unconscious on the floor, and then subsequently started the motor, the legal situation becomes very different. Dr. Devarest then met his death by accidental *means*. The fumes that actually brought about his death were those that were thrown off by the motor after it had been started by someone else."

Her eyes widened. "Donald," she exclaimed, "*how* clever! Why, that's a positive inspiration!"

"I'm glad you see what I'm driving at."

"That would get us the forty thousand dollars additional from the insurance company?"

96

"That's right."

She thought that over for a while. "Couldn't we get the insurance company to compromise by making that theory sound logical, but without going so far as to actually produce proof?"

"They won't compromise. They can't. They either have the liability or they don't. If they have it, they should pay. If they don't, they shouldn't. They'll make us fight it out. As far as they're concerned, it's double or quits."

"Why would Hilton's calls on patients have anything to do with what happened there in the garage?"

"The person who got the gems out of the glove compartment must have known they were in there."

"I see. You mean Hilton got the gems, and then the person from whom he'd received them followed him home to the garage?"

"That might have happened."

She said, "I can tell you exactly the two calls Hilton made, and they won't help you a bit."

"How do you know?" I asked.

She opened a drawer in a small bedside table, took out a leather-backed notebook. She said, "Hilton had a poor memory. He never trusted anything to his memory. He liked to do things according to system. For instance, whenever he made a call, he'd mark down the call in this notebook. The next morning his office secretary would ask for the page showing what calls he'd made. He'd take the page out of a notebook, and give it to her. In that way, he never missed a charge."

"And he marked down the calls he made the night of his death?"

"Yes. There were two. I can vouch absolutely for both patients. Both were women I know well. They are both wealthy. One is married, one a widow. They're living too hard, too many parties, too much society—at least, that's what Hilton always said. But these persons are absolutely and positively above suspicion. They're wealthy women with very real complaints. Hilton told me they both had hypertension, whatever that is."

I took the notebook and looked it over. The pages contained notes which indicated a man who didn't trust to his memory, and who was neat and efficient in his methods. He had copied out the time of high and low tide. There were tides for every Wednesday for the next six months. He had a dated page for a list of calls he'd made. There were a few telephone numbers and addresses, mostly of other doctors, evidently names he might want to call in a hurry for consultation or to assist in operations. Near the back of the book was a page with a string of figures.

"What are these?"

"We got the combination of the safe from those."

I looked at the figures and said, "Have much difficulty?"

"Some."

I thought of Dr. Devarest's type of mind, of the methodical entries in the notebook. I said, "I don't think I'd have much trouble."

She was watching me with interest. "Why not?"

"He was systematic. He trusted very little to memory. He'd be just the type to write the numbers down backward. For instance, here's eighty-four as the last number. I would say that that meant the first number to use on the combination was forty-eight."

I didn't need to ask her if I was right. I could tell it from the expression on her face.

"Donald, you're *marvelous!*"

There was surprise in her voice, but there was something in her eyes, something more than surprise. It took me a minute to place it. It was fear.

chapter 10

THE SIGN on the door read, *Forrest Timkan, Attorney and Counselor at Law—Entrance.*

I pushed open the door and walked in. Mrs. Croy was already there, waiting in the outer office. A secretary with fine red lips and lots of mascara looked up from a typewriter to ask me what I wanted. Mrs. Croy got up hastily, and said, "This is Mr. Lam. He's with me. Mr. Timkan is expecting us—both of us."

The secretary twisted the red smear into a smile, and said, "Yes, Mrs. Croy."

She walked through the door marked *Private*. I went over and sat down beside Mrs. Croy.

She frowned at the door through which the secretary had vanished. After a moment she said, half to herself, "I don't know why Timkan gets such terrible secretaries."

"What's wrong with her?" I asked. "Can't she type?"

"I don't mean that. She's—oh, obvious."

I said, "Want a cigarette?" and extended my cigarette case. She started to take one, changed her mind, and said, "No, thanks. Not now. I've made arrangements for Mr. Harmley to meet me here, and Mr. Timkan has arranged for Walter and his lawyer to come here for a conference. I told Mr. Harmley that if he'd pick me up at ten o'clock, I'd be all finished. When he comes, I'll explain that Mr. Timkan was busy and had to keep us waiting."

"How about when Walter comes in with his lawyer? Won't the relationship be slightly strained?"

She said, "Perhaps. It's been months since I've seen Walter. I wonder—"

"Yes?" I asked.

"If he's put on weight."

I lit my cigarette and settled back in a chair. "Is he inclined to put it on?"

"He has a tendency to want rich foods. I taught him self-control in his diet and he took off twenty pounds."

The door of Timkan's private office opened. Mrs. Croy said, "Here he is now. Good morning, Forrest. Mr. Timkan, this is Mr. Lam."

He shook hands with her, then with me. He was a short, nervous chap with quick, jerky motions. He had pale blue eyes and very fine, straw-colored hair that looked like imitation silk after it's been to the laundry a couple of times. He was about thirty-five, had a bulging forehead, and wore glasses. He said, "Good morning, Mr. Lam. I understand your status, of course. I'll keep up the pretext, however, that you and Mrs. Croy are very much interested in each other." He blinked at me, hesitated just long enough to make the pause emphasize his remark, then said, "*Very* much interested. I think it will be wise to seem particularly interested after Mr. Croy comes to the office."

I said, "Won't it be particularly irritating to him if he thinks his wife brought me to the legal rendezvous?"

Timkan nodded vigorously. "I hope so."

"You mean you want to irritate him?"

"It will give him something to think about. If possible, act the part of a fortune hunter—you know what I mean. You're so interested in Nadine's worldly possessions that you've attended a conference at her lawyer's office to safeguard her cash."

Nadine pouted at him and said, "Am I, then, so physically unattractive that a person who was interested in me would be labeled a fortune hunter?"

His smile held understanding and affection. "That is exactly why I wanted Mr. Lam to act as though his interest is primarily in your money. You understand, don't you, Lam?"

"I understand what you want."

"And you'll do the best you can?"

"I don't know exactly how a fortune hunter works."

"Well, just pretend that you have Mrs. Croy completely hypnotized. She's willing to marry you almost at once, and remember you're thinking of her money. And now I'll get back to my lair. Rose will flash me a signal on the buzzer when it's time for me to open the door. That will be almost at the exact moment Mr. Croy and his lawyer arrive."

He bobbed back and closed the door. We were left alone in the reception room.

Mrs. Croy settled herself in her chair, sitting so she was facing the door. She went to some pains to arrange her skirt just to suit her; then she smiled at me.

"I'm sorry, Donald. I know you must feel I'm imposing upon you, but, after all, it's really important—I mean, *very* important."

"So Harmley won't suspect that I'm a detective?"

"Well, yes—and—well, it seems like the best—"

The door opened. Harmley entered the office, stood for a moment looking around as though having some difficulty getting his eyes to focus; then he saw Mrs. Croy. He smiled and said, "Good morning— Oh, you've finished your conference. I hope I'm not late. You—"

"No," she said. "Mr. Timkan is the one that's late. I haven't even got in to see him yet. He's been busy every minute."

Harmley's eyebrows raised. "Well, I'm glad I'm not late. Good morning, Lam— I may as well wait here, I suppose." He settled down in a chair on the other side of Mrs. Croy.

The door of Timkan's private office opened, and the secretary came bustling out, carrying a handful of legal papers which she placed in various piles on her desk. She said "Good morning" to Harmley and asked his name.

Mrs. Croy said, "He's with me."

She smiled. "Mr. Timkan wanted me to tell you how sorry he was. He'll see you in just a few minutes."

She settled herself in her stenographic chair, whipped paper and carbon paper out of her desk, fed the paper into the machine with a great show of frenzied haste, then opened a drawer in her desk, took out a mirror and lipstick, and began touching up her mouth.

The entrance door opened, and two men came in. I took one swift look, then turned to watch Harmley and

Mrs. Croy.

Mrs. Croy tilted her chin, lowered her eyes demurely. Harmley glanced up, then casually looked over toward Mrs. Croy and said, "He must be pretty busy."

She didn't answer him. She raised her eyes and said, with synthetic sweetness, "Good morning, Walter."

The men were closer now. Harmley surveyed them as they swung toward us. There was just the faint interest of a well-bred curiosity in his glance, no more.

Mrs. Croy said, "Donald, this is Walter Croy."

I got up and met a pair of hostile gray eyes, glanced down and saw that Harmley was looking, not at Walter, but at me. There was a quizzical expression on his face.

Walter Croy had evidently put the twenty pounds back on. He said, "Good morning, Mr. Lam. How you been, Nadine? This is my lawyer, Mr. Pinchley."

Pinchley was tall, broad-shouldered, rather good-looking in a heavy-featured sort of a way, but didn't seem particularly quick on the trigger. Mrs. Croy introduced Harmley, and then the door of Timkan's office opened, and he was standing, bowing, greeting everyone, and apologizing all at once. The explanations were reasonable. The apologies were profuse; but the effect of the whole thing was that he was talking too fast and too much.

Nadine Croy said, "Now, Donald, you be a dear and wait here. And you won't mind waiting just a few moments, will you, Mr. Harmley? You and Donald can talk with each other."

She turned to her former husband. "Walter, you're looking fine, *marvelously* well!"

He smiled down at her. His face had the same expression it would have worn if he'd been regarding a talkative, interesting, but dangerously mischievous child. "I'm afraid I've put on a little weight," he said.

"Oh, have you, Walter? Why, I just thought that you looked *so* well. I see now you're a little heavier, but—"

Timkan said, "Won't you come in, please?"

They filed on into Timkan's private office, and left Harmley and me sitting there together.

When the door closed, Harmley leaned toward me so his low-voiced conversation wouldn't be audible to Timkan's secretary, and said, "What does her husband do?"

"I don't know."

He looked at me again with that peculiarly puzzled expression.

I said, "She rarely talks about her husband. Was there some particular reason why you were interested?"

"Yes. I've told you that I had the impression I'd met Mrs. Croy somewhere before. I have the same feeling about her husband."

"Is that so?"

"Yes. I didn't realize it at first. It was just as he went through that door into Mr. Timkan's private office that it flashed on my mind there was something familiar about the man's walk, the way he carried his shoulders. I have a wretched memory for people and associations. That is, I can remember vaguely having seen them, but I can't recall the circumstances."

"Many people are like that."

"Are you that way?"

"No."

"I wish I weren't. I'd give almost anything to be able to recall people and names and associations."

"Perhaps you met them somewhere while they were living together."

"I must have. There's a vague feeling of uneasiness in the back of my mind as though my memory were trying to warn me about some past experience which was unpleasant." He glanced at me and then added hastily, "Not, you understand, so far as Mrs. Croy is concerned. I've simply felt that I've met her somewhere before, but as the impression that I've known her husband returns to me, there's the feeling that—well, that I'd just escaped being trimmed in some business deal."

"You can't remember what it was?"

"No. That's just the point."

"You can't think of anything that would give you a clue?"

"No. And I haven't been able to recall anything significant in my last conversation with Dr. Devarest."

We sat silent for a while. I could hear the hum of voices from Timkan's private office; then, after four or five minutes, Mrs. Croy came through the door. She swept in, clothed in an invisible aura of self-satisfied triumph.

She smiled at Harmley, walked around him to lean over close to my ear. "You'll forgive me, Mr. Harmley, if I whisper. It's a minor matter, and yet it may be very—very important."

"Certainly. I'll leave, if you wish to have a conference in private, and—"

"No, no, nothing like that. I just wanted you to understand."

She placed an intimate hand on my shoulder, leaned forward so her lips were within an inch of my ear, and whispered, "Oh, Donald, it's working so wonderfully well! I'm so elated. He's furious about you. You be sure to wait right here. Don't go away, no matter what happens. Do you know, Donald, I really believe we're going to put it across. We've got him completely fooled this time. And he's not an easy man to fool."

I said, "That's fine."

She whispered even less audibly, with her lips almost brushing my ear, "He's made a proposition. I told him I'd have to think it over, and then came out to see you. That's the thing that's irritating him more than anything else, the fact that you're sitting out here and really having the final say in our conference."

I said, "Yes. I can readily understand."

She laughed, raised her right hand from my shoulder to pat my cheek. "You boys wait right here. It won't be long now."

Harmley said dubiously, "My experience has been that conferences of this kind, where two lawyers and two clients are together, usually take a long time."

She said, "Oh, I'm quite sure this will be over in a few minutes." Then she hesitated. "Really, however, I've imposed on you frightfully."

"Not at all."

"I had someone I wanted you to meet, a friend of Dr. Devarest. He's terribly interested in you."

Harmley said, "I should like very much to meet him."

"I don't like to ask you to wait. It's unfortunate that Mr. Timkan was so busy he couldn't keep his appointment with me."

Harmley pinched his eyebrows together thoughtfully, looked at his wrist watch, suddenly got up and said, "Really, my dear, I'm afraid this is going to take much longer than you anticipate. I have an appointment in half an hour that I simply must keep. Even if you finish this conference within the next few minutes, and I were to meet some friend of Dr. Devarest—well, you know how it would be. I'd hate to shake hands, and then dash off."

"Yes, that would be unfortunate."

"Suppose we postpone it until tomorrow or next day."

"Well—yes, I guess that's best."

"I think so."

Impulsively she gave him her hand, came to stand close to him, looking up at his face. "You've been perfectly splendid, Mr. Harmley. I can understand just how my uncle felt about you, and when I think of how I've inconvenienced you, I feel terribly ashamed. It really wasn't my fault, but—well, you can see the way things happened."

"Certainly. It was something you couldn't have controlled in the least. I appreciate that perfectly."

"Thank you so much then, and good-by."

"Good-by. I'll see you later on."

He left the office, and Nadine Croy came over to me again. She leaned over, breathed in my ear, "You're doing splendidly, Donald. Did he show any sign of recognition?"

"No. But afterward the situation was slightly different. I have something to tell you when you're at liberty."

She gave the upper part of my arm a gentle squeeze, and favored me with a smile of what seemed studied invitation before vanishing through the door to the inner office once more.

The secretary was looking at me thoughtfully.

I sat for another ten minutes, then abruptly the door opened, and Walter Croy and his lawyer came out. Timkan followed them as far as the outer office. "You understand how it is," he said. "No hard feelings, but—"

"We'll let you know tomorrow," Croy's lawyer said, and marched his client through the door. Croy flashed me one sidelong glance, then the door closed, and Timkan was beckoning me to his private office.

I went in. Timkan asked anxiously, "Did he give any sign of recognition?"

"Not at the time. But he told me that, as he watched Croy enter your office, he thought he'd seen him before—says he can't place him—says there's a feeling in the back of his mind that the association was disagreeable, thinks he might almost have been trimmed in a business deal. Does that mean anything to you?"

Timkan looked at Mrs. Croy, frowned, walked over to the window, stood looking down at the traffic, then turned back to me and said, "It all fits in. If we could find some way of jogging his memory, he could probably give us the key clue. But I don't see how he could have given Dr. Devarest information that was a stranglehold on Walter Croy, and yet not have known what the information was, or be able to recall it now."

I said, "I didn't think Croy showed any sign of recognizing him."

"No," Nadine Croy said. "I'm quite certain he didn't."

"I take it, however, that Walter Croy wasn't as hard to handle as you'd anticipated."

Timkan said, "That's right."

I said, "Has it ever occurred to you Walter may be a better actor than we give him credit for?"

"What do you mean?" Timkan asked.

I said, "Suppose he recognized Harmley as soon as he saw him, but realized Harmley didn't recognize him. He knew that Harmley would place him sooner or later, so decided to make hay while the sun was shining, get the best settlement he could, and get out from under."

Timkan thought that over. "There's something to that—only he wasn't quite that tractable."

"Then I misunderstood you. I thought things were going satisfactorily."

"Not on the money end," Mrs. Croy said, and then sucked in her breath as though she wished to recall the words.

Timkan scowled.

I said, "I'm not trying to pry into your business. I was just making a suggestion. Can I do anything else?"

She looked at him, and I could see there was relief in his eyes at getting rid of me without having to make some excuse. She turned to me with her sweetest smile. "No, Donald, you've been splendid—wonderful. If you have something to do, run right along."

I stopped in the outer office for my hat. The secretary quit typing to look up at me speculatively. Then she glanced impatiently at the closed door to Timkan's private office.

Faraday Foster, the consulting criminologist, had offices in the building across the street. I made certain no one was taking an undue interest in what I was doing, and then crossed the street and went up to his office.

Foster was a good example of the modern, scientific detective. He looked like a college professor.

I gave him my card, and said, "I want to find out something about these hairs."

He took the hairs from the small envelope I handed him, looked them over, said, "All right, come with me."

His laboratory was an elaborate affair. I saw a comparison microscope, a device for impregnating paper with vapors for testing invisible ink, an ultraviolet-ray photographic outfit, microphotographic equipment, and a binocular microscope.

"Want to sit over here and smoke?" he asked. "Or check on things as I go along?"

"I'd prefer to check as you go along."

"Then come on over here."

He took the hairs, one at a time, spread them on a sheet of glass; then put a drop of cement at two points along the hair to hold it rigid. He slid the glass slide under a microscope, and for several seconds twisted a focusing knob back and forth. Then he began handing out comments. "These hairs weren't cut. They were pulled out. The bulbs show a slight atrophy at the roots. There's a complete absence of sheath. I'd say this hair I'm looking at now came from a woman about forty to forty-five—well, make it thirty-five to fifty to be on the safe side. The hair probably came out with very little pressure. I would say it might have been found on a comb or on a brush."

"Are they all the same?" I asked.

He studied the slide through his microscope. "No."

"Well, what can you tell me about the others?"

He said, "Just a minute. I want to check on this."

He snipped off bits from the ends of the hairs, put them in a machine, and gradually turned a wheel. Bits of hair so fine it was almost impossible to see them dropped to a glass slide. He put a cover glass over this slide, and inserted it in another microscope. He studied these pieces for a while, then went back to the binocular microscope. "Want to take a look, Lam?" he asked.

I moved over to the big binocular microscope, placed my eyes up to the eyepieces, and seemed to be staring at a piece of Manila rope about a half inch in diameter.

Foster asked, "Do you get the effect of seeing certain distinctive bits of structure in that hair through a peculiar reddish haze?"

"Well—"

"Here, take a look at this. It will show you what I mean."

He moved the slide a little, and the reddish hemp rope gave way to a jet-black wire cable. "Take a look at this. There's a peculiar structure on the outside of the hair, a scale structure like rough bark on a tree. Do you see it?"

"Yes."

"All right. Now take a look at the same structure on this hair. Get it?"

Once more, the Manila-rope-like hair was in my field of vision.

"I get it."

"See that reddish haze? It's like looking through a sheet of orange glass."

"What does it mean?"

"A dye," he said. "Probably a henna rinse."

"Then you have hairs from at least two persons here."

"More than two. You have given me five hair specimens. I would say they came from at least three different women."

"Can you tell me any more about them?"

"Not definitely, and not now. I'm making only a superficial examination at present. If you really want a detailed report, I'll wash the hairs in equal parts of ether and rectified spirit. Then I'll dry them, treat them with oil of turpentine, mount them on slides, and make a really detailed examination. I can tell you more at that time. How much more, I don't know."

"How long will that take?"

"About forty-eight hours to get the complete report."

"That's too long."

"Does what I have given you help you any?"

"Quite a bit, yes."

"Do you want me to go ahead with the tests?"

I said, "Mount the hairs on slides so you can identify them as hairs you received from me, and number them as specimens one, two, three, four, and five. We may have use for them later on. I'll let you know."

I drove to headquarters. Lieutenant Lisman was glad to see me. He pumped my hand up and down, clapped me on the back, puffed smoke from a Perfecto in my face, and said, "It's a real pleasure to work with an intelligent private detective. So damn many chaps in the business don't know which side of the bread has the butter. You can't depend on them to give you a damn thing except a bum steer."

"You got results on the tip-off?" I asked him.

"Did I!"

"You didn't let her know where it came from?"

"Of course not. We always protect our sources of information. Look here, Lam, you and I can do business. It's a pleasure to encourage private detectives who want to co-operate."

"That's swell. What did the Starr woman have to say?"

"Not very much. That's the interesting part. She says she left the way she did because Dr. Devarest tried to take advantage of her position."

"Oh-oh."

"What's more, she sticks with it."

"Any of the sordid details?" I asked.

"Lots of them. A whole series of advances, getting up to the point where he had courage enough to make passes at her, then putting on the pressure."

"It's a story that would sound well in front of a jury."

"Yes," he admitted, "a jury would be a pushover for that sort of stuff. The widow naturally wouldn't want it made public."

"Think that's an accident?"

"What is?"

"When she shows up, she has such a nice tear-jerker alibi."

"Well," he said thoughtfully, "of course—"

"I see you've already given consideration to that theory," I said.

"What theory?"

"That a smart lawyer thought it up for her."

He twisted his cigar around in his lips, thought it over for a while, and said, "It's a tailor-made story. It fits her and the situation like a glove, and yet I don't believe it. I can't find a weak place in it, but I'm satisfied it's there. Dammit, Lam, a lawyer *did* think up that story."

"Going to hold her?"

"Just long enough for one of the deputy D.A.s to get a statement. We've nothing against her so far. The skip-out was the thing that made us look for her."

"She didn't tell Mrs. Devarest anything about it?"

"No. When he started pawing, she stood it as long as she could, and then walked out."

"And never even went back for her toothbrush?"

Lisman frowned and said, "It is fishy as hell, isn't it, Lam?"

"Uh huh."

"The more you think of it, the more phony it sounds. The idea of the old guy finding out his jewels were gone, and then stopping to make a pass at his wife's secretary."

"This one, I take it, was passier than the others?"

"That's right."

"Evidently the lost gems didn't concern him very much."

"No. Somehow, you can't feature Devarest discovering

111

the theft, and then taking time out for a little dalliance. You'd think he'd have been hot-footing it to get the police on the phone."

I nodded.

"But if that's the case, why didn't he call himself? Why expect this Nollie Starr to handle it?"

"There are two answers to that. Both of them are deep."

"How deep?"

"Under six feet of earth."

He thought that over, then moved his head up and down with a slowly thoughtful motion of assent. Apparently he was entirely oblivious of my presence for the moment. It was only after I coughed that he seemed to remember I was there.

"How would you like to tell me something?" I asked.

"Fine."

"How about your systems of identification?"

"Fingerprint classifications? You get them in the form of fractions, and—"

"That isn't what I want. I want the other classifications."

"We have *modus operandi*, signs, and physical peculiarities."

"Would you have a file of physical peculiarities?"

"Well, not exactly that, but, for instance, if a man had one thumb missing, we'd have a file of crooks with missing thumbs. It's a mean piece of card indexing, and I'm not certain that it's worth what it cost. But occasionally it's a veritable gold mine."

"For instance, then, if a man had a scar on his chin— say a scar which might have been made by a knife wound —you'd have him listed?"

"Uh huh."

I said, "I think it'd be a swell idea for me to take a look at that file. I'd like to browse around in it a little while."

"Why, are you on the track of something?"

"No. I'm trying to familiarize myself with police methods of investigation. Do I find everyone who has the same physical peculiarities listed under a file, whether they're housebreakers, stick-up men, or confidence men?"

"That's right."

"Would it be too much of a job for you to let me take a look at that file?"

"What are you looking for specifically?"

"Men with deep scars in the middle of the chin."

He said, "Okay, come this way."

He led me down a corridor, through a steel door into a room which bristled with filing-cases. He said, "We're way ahead of any department in the country on this sort of stuff, but we don't get enough credit for it. It's hard to get funds to keep it up."

"It must take a lot of work."

"It does."

He stopped in front of a steel file that was marked, *Scars on Head*. He pulled out a drawer. There were subdivisions. *Scars on left side of face. Scars on right side of face. Scars on nose. Scars on chin. Scars on forehead.*

He pulled out a section of cards. "Don't mix these up," he said.

"I won't," I promised.

He looked at his watch. "I've got to be on my way. If anybody asks any questions, tell them Lieutenant Lisman brought you in here."

"Okay, Lieutenant, thanks."

After he'd gone, I shoved back the cards and pulled out the section I wanted. There weren't a great number of cards in it. I picked out four names and identifying file-card numbers.

A couple of other officers were in the place. Lieutenant Lisman's name and the file numbers of the cards brought me the information on how to find what I wanted. The first two cards didn't mean anything. The third card had the face of Rufus Bayley looking up at me. *Paul Rufus, alias Rufus Paul, alias Rufus Cutting. Works exclusively on safes and gems. At one time worked a confidence racket. Plays a lone hand. Has few accomplices, confederates, or confidants. Has a way with women, and frequently uses an affair with a servant to get him the information he wants and the opportunity to use it. Age, twenty-nine. Criminal record consists of one term in Sing Sing when caught red-handed working on a safe. Had used a maid to act as lookout. She became irritated over other philanderings and tipped off police. Prisoner suspected treachery, although never had any confirmation from police. Arrested half a dozen times, but keeps a close mouth when interrogated, and because he has no confidants, police have been unable to make any other case against him stick.*

Fingerprint classifications, Bertillon measurements, and detailed record on reverse side.

I turned over to the back of the card and made a series of notes covering the high lights of the somewhat meager information and data assembled there.

I figured my next stop might well be the Devarest house.

chapter 11

RUFUS BAYLEY CAME IN after I'd been waiting about half an hour. He gave me his toothy grin.

I strolled over to the garage.

"Suppose you could get those sparklers for me?"

"Sparklers!"

"That's right."

"What would I be doing getting any sparklers for you?"

"Oh, I thought you might accommodate a friend."

"Buddy, you're talking a language I don't know anything about."

I looked up at the room over the garage and said, "Those Venetian blinds certainly are nice."

"Uh huh."

"Let in the wind and ventilation, and you can have

sunlight when you want."

"Uh huh."

"And by putting them at the right angle, it's absolutely impossible for anyone to see what's going on in the room above."

"Well now, ain't you the smart boy?"

"And a new bed gets moved in about the time the Venetian blinds were put on."

"You're saying a lot of words."

"Makes the place very nice and comfortable up there. Must be a lot different from Sing Sing."

The smile came off his face. For a moment there was a hot glitter in his eyes; then the grin was back once more, and he said easily, "Oh, so you know that too, do you?"

"That's right."

"Been reading my mail?"

"Uh huh."

"What do you want?"

"The sparklers."

"Buddy, I'm going to tell you something. I laid off the racket, see? I was pretty good at it, but what does it get you? In the first place, you're just working for a bunch of fences. You can't move the swag without having a hook-up with some fence. You get ten thousand dollars' worth of ice; the victim squawks it's a fifty-thousand-dollar job; the fence pays you about a grand for the whole works. You work your head off to make eight or ten grand a year for yourself, and get as hot as a baked potato doing it. Even then the government can pull a Capone on you, and send you to the big rock for failing to pay your income taxes. After I took that jolt, I did a lot of thinking. I like lots of things you can't get in jail. I don't like jails. I want food that ain't all doped up with saltpeter. I want elbow room. I like driving cars. I like lots of things they don't give you in jails."

I said, "Yes. Your room gives evidences of that. I took

a sample of hairs from the brush on the dressing-table. You'd be surprised at what a good criminologist can tell about human hair."

He looked at me for nearly ten seconds before he said, "I try to get along with people, but I'm not so certain you and I are going to be real buddies."

"I'm after just one thing."

"What's that?"

"The sparklers."

"I tell you I ain't got them."

"That's right."

"What is?"

"That you've told me you haven't got them."

"Okay, I've told you I haven't got them, and I haven't got them. Now what?"

"How about getting them?"

"I wouldn't know where to look."

"Think it over, and you might."

He turned around to study me carefully. "You sing a funny song," he said. "Who's writing the lyrics?"

"I am."

"I don't like 'em."

"It has different verses," I told him.

"But the chorus is always the same."

I said, "Jim Timley was calling at Nollie Starr's apartment when I dropped in. Nollie Starr has a roommate, girl by the name of Dorothy Grail. Jim Timley was supposed to be calling on the Grail girl, supposed to be a steady of hers."

"Keep talking," Bayley said. "You're beginning to say something besides just words now."

I said, "Timley kissed Dorothy Grail good night. He didn't act as though he'd ever kissed her before."

"How so?"

"He got a surprise."

I saw Bayley's eyes light up. "High voltage?"

"That's right."

"What was the idea?"

"Oh, I think she'd seen him several times before, but he hadn't seen her. She thought she'd let him know she wasn't inanimate. I think maybe she gets a kick out of teasing the animals. When you're good at something, and know you're good, you like to keep your hand in."

He thought that over. "What kind is this Dorothy Grail?"

"Class. Not too old, not too young, not too fat, not too skinny. To put it mildly, she's all right and when she kisses you good night, she gives a little wiggle."

"Hot dog!" Bayley said.

"When Timley started home, Nollie Starr handed him a package."

"What kind of a package?"

"Done up in brown paper. It was supposed to be books."

"Where does this Starr girl hang out?"

"681 East Bendon Street. The apartment's in the name of Dorothy Grail."

"What is this Grail girl, blonde or brunette?"

"Brunette."

"How's her face, pretty?"

"She isn't a doll. She has character."

"She sounds interesting. When would you be wanting those sparklers?"

"As soon as I could get them."

"No questions asked?"

"By me, yes."

He said, "I'll think things over."

"Don't think too long."

"You put me on a spot. I'm getting along pretty well here. There's a chance I might fall into something real soft."

"Not if the bulls should tell her about your record. As far as they're concerned, your record plus the missing

117

jewels might just happen to add up to the answer in the back of the book."

"When did you get those hairs out of the brush?"

"When I got you to go in the closet to check up on that scarf. You didn't do so good on that, you know—picking a scarf up out of the automobile and taking it up to your bedroom to find out to whom it belonged."

"I should have taken it out of the bedroom."

"You should."

"Would tonight be all right?"

"If it isn't after midnight."

He said, "I don't know just what's going to be going on."

"I want to get some barometric data. I think there's going to be another east wind tonight. The sky's a black blue. You can see the mountains standing out almost in your front yard."

"That's right. There's lots of electricity in my hair. I can usually tell from that."

"Been brushing it?"

"Uh huh."

"With the brush on the dressing-table?"

He grinned and said, "No. The other one."

I said, "I'm ringing up the weather bureau a little later on. If there's going to be an east wind tonight, you might have plenty of chances to move around."

"What's the east wind got to do with it?"

"I've been thinking about Dr. Devarest's death. If he didn't have the garage door all the way up when he drove in, a sudden gust of wind could have blown it shut."

"What difference does it make how the door got closed?"

"Only forty thousand dollars."

"How come?"

"A sudden gust of wind of unusual severity would have been an accidental means within the meaning of the insurance policy."

"I'm not certain I get you, buddy."

"I'm not certain I'm supposed to tell you, anyway."

"Then why open it up?"

"Because it might mean you'd have lots of chances to move around."

"Okay, buddy. I'll see what I can do. It's a deal."

"Not a deal. I was just telling you something I wanted."

"If it's like that, what's to keep you from wanting something else later on?"

I looked him straight in the eye and said, "Nothing."

"You drive a hard bargain. You know, buddy, if I was in the life insurance business, I think I'd cancel you out as a bad risk."

"You wouldn't have had to pay any losses on any policy —up to now."

"Up to now," he repeated as though turning over the effect of the words in his mind.

"By midnight tonight then," I said, and walked away.

I walked across from the garage over to the back door of the house. There was a small brass sign marked *Tradesmen*. Under it was a bell. I pushed the bell button. After a while, Jeanette, the maid, opened the door wearing that expression of haughty disdain which the servants of a wealthy family assume for house-to-house solicitors.

I could see the expression change. Surprise—a flicker of fear perhaps—then red lips parting to show some pretty nice teeth.

"Oh, it's you!"

Her voice indicated she was glad.

"Mrs. Devarest home?"

She pouted. "Did you want to see her?"

"Yes. Why?"

"You don't have to come to the back door to see her. I thought—perhaps you wanted to see someone else."

She lowered her lids until her long lashes showed to advantage against her cheeks, then snapped her eyes open, and glanced at me coquettishly.

I said, "I did."

"Oh."

"Is anyone in Miss Starr's room?"

"No."

"I want to take another look at it."

"Will you come this way, please?"

She was very efficient as she guided me through the kitchen and into the wing which contained the servants' rooms, but after I entered the room Nollie Starr had occupied, she followed me in, closed the door, and stood with her back against it, her eyes taking in every move I made.

"Was there anything else you wanted?"

"No."

Her eyes followed me as I looked around the room.

"Of course, I'm not supposed to know what's going on," she said, "but—are you getting anywhere?"

"I think so."

"Didn't you—didn't I see you going up to Rufus Bayley's rooms over the garage?"

"You may have."

"Are you—I mean have you been—"

I grinned and said, "Yes."

She colored and lowered her eyes.

"Who makes the beds?" I asked.

"He makes his own."

"I don't mean Bayley's. I mean down here."

"Oh, the housekeeper."

I said, "Nollie Starr left on Tuesday. On Wednesday, Dr. Devarest called me in. Wednesday evening I came down to look this room over. I found the alarm clock wound. I wonder if the bed had been slept in. You didn't see Miss Starr come back here Tuesday night, did you?"

"No."

"Or know that she occupied her room?"

She was fidgeting now. "No," she said, avoiding my eyes.

"You don't know who slept in her room?"

"No."

She raised her eyes to mine, lowered them. She walked over to stand beside me, put her hand on my arm. Her touch was a caressing gesture. "Did Rufus say anything—about me?"

"Why should he?"

She was standing close to me now, still holding my arm. I could feel the rounded curve of her breast against my biceps. She said, "Things get terribly dull for us here. We are only permitted to go out one night a week. When we know we're not going to be wanted, we—well, we have our good times together, sometimes a little to drink, and—well, you know how it is."

"So what?"

"Don't tell Mrs. Devarest everything you find out."

"Why not?"

Her eyes met mine steadily. "Because she's absolutely crazy about Rufus, and she's insanely jealous."

"How about Nollie Starr? Did she get in on any of your parties?"

"No. She wasn't exactly one of us."

I said, "I'm going in to see Mrs. Devarest."

"The doctor's in there."

"Dr. Gelderfield?"

"Yes."

"How long's he been treating her?"

"Oh, a year or so. Dr. Devarest was treating Dr. Gelderfield's father, so he called Dr. Gelderfield for his wife."

"And Nollie Starr didn't mix in on your parties?"

"No."

"But she found it rather tedious being chained to the house six nights a week?"

"I don't know. I never discussed it with her."

"What did she do in the evenings?"

Jeannette tried to avoid my eyes and the question.

"What did she do in the evenings?" I repeated. "Where

did she spend her time?"

"In her room, I guess."

"Did you ever see her light here?"

"Oh, yes—sometimes."

"Mrs. Devarest usually retired early?"

"Yes. There's something wrong with her heart. Dr. Gelderfield's been quite worried."

"He's in with her now?"

She nodded.

"I'm going in."

She kept clinging to my arm. "You won't say anything to Mrs. Devarest about—about me?"

"What is there to say?"

She couldn't think of the answer to that one. I gently freed my arm and left the room.

Dr. Gelderfield was sitting in the library with Mrs. Devarest. He'd ordered a wheel chair for her. She was sitting in it, enjoying being an invalid. They looked up as I came in.

Mrs. Devarest said, "Why, Donald, I didn't know you were here."

"I've been around for a while."

Dr. Gelderfield said, "Well, I must be going, Colette. I don't think there's anything you need be alarmed about, only keep quiet and ring me up if that medicine doesn't help."

"You're so considerate, Warren. I don't know how I'm ever going to thank you."

He said, "I only wish there was more I could do. You don't realize how much Hilton did for me."

He turned to me and said, "I think that attitude of the insurance company is the damnedest thing I ever encountered. How are you doing, Lam?"

"Making progress."

Dr. Gelderfield turned so that Mrs. Devarest could only see the left side of his face. He said, "Mrs. Devarest has had a nervous shock. She's recovering very nicely, but I don't want anything to happen that would undo the good we're accomplishing." His right eye closed in a slow wink, then he jerked his head toward the door.

Mrs. Devarest smiled and said, "Don't make Donald think I'm decrepit, Warren." She arched a smile and waited for my compliment.

I said, "I had always assumed you were Dr. Devarest's second wife because you looked so much younger. I only found out recently that there had only been one Mrs. Devarest."

"Donald, are you flattering me?"

"Simply stating a fact, my dear," Dr. Gelderfield said. "Well, I must be on my way. By the way, Lam, how did you come out? On the streetcar?"

Once more, his eye closed in a slow wink.

"Yes."

"Going my way? I'll give you a lift."

I said, "That will be fine."

"But, Donald, didn't you have something to report?"

I nodded.

She said, "Go right ahead. I have no secrets from my physician."

He laughed and said, "Few patients do, but lots of them *think* they have."

I said, "I think there's going to be an east wind tonight."

"Well?"

I said, "You'll remember the night Dr. Devarest died there was one of those desert east winds that came sweeping down to strike with a blast."

"Well, what's that got to do with it?"

I said, "There are counterweights on those doors to make it easy to raise and lower them. The door through which Dr. Devarest drove his car had a rope that was supposed to hang down from a lever on the inside of the garage, so that, if necessary, the door could be closed from the inside of the garage. That rope was tangled up so it couldn't be reached. That fact shows very plainly in the photographs."

"You've mentioned something like that before, Donald. What does it mean?"

I said, "It means either that Dr. Devarest opened the garage door, drove into the garage, walked out, closed the garage door, opened one of the other doors enough to go into the garage, and then started tinkering with his motor; or it means that when he raised the door to drive in, he knew there wasn't any rope by which he could pull it closed. That might mean he didn't open the door all the way."

"But he'd have to," Mrs. Devarest said. "Those doors slide up and down and—"

"No. There's a point of balance at which the counterweight just equally balances the weight of the door, and if you put the door in that position, it will stay there."

"Have you experimented?"

"Yes."

"And what's your theory?" Dr. Gelderfield asked.

I said, "The east wind struck with considerable violence. The door was on a point of balance. The wind upset that balance and blew the door shut."

"I don't see what difference that makes," Mrs. Devarest said. "What do we care how it got shut?"

"Because in one case the *means* of death weren't accidental. In another, they were."

"You mean the wind would be—"

"An accidental means," I said.

Gelderfield said, "I'm afraid I don't get you."

"In the one instance," I pointed out, "every factor that contributed to his death was set in motion by the decedent. In the other event, a sudden, unusual gust of wind furnished an intervening cause."

"You mean you could stick the insurance company?"

"Exactly."

Dr. Gelderfield was excited. "How would you go about doing it?"

I said, "I'm waiting for another east wind. I think there's going to be one tonight. I've telephoned the weather bureau. It thinks so, too."

"And you'll conduct an experiment?"

"Yes."

Mrs. Devarest said, "Won't that be wonderful if—"

Dr. Gelderfield regarded her with professional concentration. "I'm not certain you should be there, Colette. It would be rather exciting—something of a strain. And if there should be a disappointment—if the wind isn't strong enough to blow the door—well, that would be quite a letdown."

"Oh, Warren, I want to be there."

Dr. Gelderfield looked at his watch. "Well—what time do you intend to make this experiment, Lam?"

"Whenever the east wind strikes. I can get a report from the weather bureau which will fix the time within half an hour or so."

Dr. Gelderfield gnawed at his upper lip. "Very well," he said, suddenly reaching a decision. "I'll try and be here. If I'm here, Colette, you can watch the experiment from your wheel chair. If I'm not, you'd better learn what happens from some of the others. Remember now—*no stairs!*"

She pouted archly at him. "I want to see it, Warren."

"Have you any idea what time the wind will strike, Lam?" he asked.

"The weather bureau thinks about nine o'clock."

"I'll try and make it," Gelderfield said with his most magnetic professional smile. Then he turned to me. "All ready, Lam—if you are."

I followed him out to his car.

"Where's your bus parked?"

"About a block away."

"I didn't see it here as I drove up."

"I seldom leave it in front of the house. I just wanted to tell you something about Colette's condition. She thinks it's merely a nerve shock. It's more serious."

"How serious?" I asked.

He said, "Dr. Devarest didn't want her told."

"What is it?" I asked.

He said somewhat sternly, "It's a matter that needn't concern you. I simply wanted you to know the general situation. I don't want her to have any severe shock. If you find anything that might be startling or which might make her angry, you'd better tell me before you break the news to her, and let me pick an auspicious moment—from a physical standpoint, I mean."

"What do you mean—anything which might make her mad?"

He met my eyes. "The fact that Dr. Devarest was leading a double life."

"Do you know such was the case?"

"I rather suspected."

"And have for some time?" I asked.

"That also," he said, "is a matter that lies entirely outside the scope of your inquiry. I'll telephone the weather bureau and keep posted. If I'm there, she may watch the test, but under no circumstances is she to do so unless I am there. I may have to give her a hypodermic rather quickly."

"That about making her angry," I said. "Does that apply to anything other than news of her husband's philandering?"

He got into his automobile, drew on his driving-gloves. "Anger would be the worst thing on earth for her. Worry would be next to it. Those two mental states must be avoided at any cost."

"Jubilation?" I asked. "Triumph? Or—"

"Anger and worry," he said. "I'm trying to protect her as much as I can. I'm looking to you to help."

"There's no chance of effecting a permanent cure?"

He met my eye. "I see no reason for telling you anything except that she is to be spared anger and worry. If you uncover anything about Dr. Devarest's affairs, you had better come to me. I think you understand the situation. Good day."

"I'll see you later?"

"I'm going to try to make it."

"She wants to be there to see what happens."

"I'm not certain that I want her there, certainly not unless I'm on the job."

"When this east wind strikes, I have to be ready. I can't postpone it."

"I understand."

"How well," I asked, "did you know Dr. Devarest?"

His eyes searched mine. "Why do you ask?"

"Getting back to that double life idea," I said.

"What about it?"

"Did you have Nollie Starr in mind as the third point in the triangle?"

He thought that over, then said simply, "Yes."

"And you know something which makes that conclusion seem logical?"

"Yes."

"What?"

He shook his head.

I said, "It might be important."

"Doubtless, it is," he said dryly.

"Look here, Doctor, there's no use fencing at arm's length. Either we're working on the same side of the case, or we're not. It looks to me as though we are."

"Well?"

"You're rather uncommunicative."

"I see no reason for telling you anything other than what I already have."

I said, "All right, I'll tell you. I've found Nollie Starr.

She's at 681 East Bendon Street. The apartment's under the name of Dorothy Grail. I went up to call on her. I found Jim Timley there. I think Timley is sweet on Nollie Starr. They tried to make it look as though Dorothy Grail was the one he was interested in. Now does *that* mean anything to you?"

Dr. Gelderfield closed his eyes as though to shut me out of his mind while he gave the matter consideration. After a few moments, he said, "It might," then added, "I sincerely hope so."

I said, "The way I look at it, if Timley, who is under Mrs. Devarest's thumb, took a healthy interest in Nollie Starr, the domestic situation might have become complicated. There's a possibility Dr. Devarest was wise to the situation, knew what was going on, and approved of it."

Dr. Gelderfield said in a sudden burst of confidence, with relief in his voice, "My God, Lam, I hope you're right! All I know is that Devarest was supposed to have been at the hospital at six o'clock on an appendicitis operation. He wasn't there. I happened to have been at the hospital myself on an emergency, and know he wasn't in. About seven o'clock, I was driving past one of the parks, and I saw Devarest and Nollie Starr playing tennis. Neither one of them saw me. I thought perhaps—well, that it might have been the windup of a party that had started quite a bit earlier."

"Anything else?" I asked.

"A couple of times Dr. Devarest mentioned that he had been called out at night, and the little notebook in which he kept notations for his professional charges didn't show that he had made any visits."

"Now you're getting close to something that I want."

"What?"

"How much chance is there that Dr. Devarest might have made calls from time to time and not entered them in that book?"

He shook his head. "No chance whatever—not unless it was done deliberately. Devarest was nuts on system. He had everything systematized. Why do you ask?"

"It occurs to me that he might have made a call on the night he died that wasn't listed in his book."

"What makes you think that?"

"He might have called on someone who knew something about what had been taken from the safe."

"You mean the jewels?"

"No, something other than the jewels. The call might have come to him as though it were a patient calling for a doctor. Dr. Devarest would have answered it on that assumption."

Once more, Gelderfield closed his eyes. "It's an interesting possibility," he said, "but I don't think—well, you *may* be right."

"You wouldn't know of any way to help me find out?"

He shook his head.

I said, "There's some possibility Nollie Starr might help me there."

He gave that matter grave consideration, then nodded, said, "You may be on the track of something."

I said, "Mrs. Devarest feels that the two calls which are listed in his notebook couldn't possibly have had anything to do with—"

He interrupted me by nodding his head vehemently. "I know all about both cases," he said. "I've taken those patients over since Dr. Devarest's death. There's not a possibility."

"Then he must have made some visit that he didn't enter in his book."

Gelderfield said, "That's hardly possible, either."

"Well, I'm going to keep plugging away."

Abruptly, Dr. Gelderfield's hand shot out across the door of the car and gripped mine. "I'm afraid I've been a little prejudiced against private investigators," he said, "but I realize now that you have brains and are using them. Call on me for anything I can do to help."

It was a sudden change of front. Watching him whisk his car away from the curb, I flexed my hand to make sure the knuckles weren't crushed. "You didn't need to be so damn enthusiastic about it," I said to the departing license plate on his automobile. "I *might* want to use that hand again sometime."

chapter 12

IN THE DARKNESS, we made a group as we stood around in front of the garage. Dr. Gelderfield had placed Mrs. Devarest in a wheel chair and covered her with robes. Bertha Cool, looking hard and competent, surveyed the group with a keen, hard eye.

Mrs. Devarest had invited Corbin Harmley, or he had tactfully invited himself—I never quite found out which. Probably Mrs. Devarest herself wouldn't have known. Harmley had that deft tact by which he could get exactly what he wanted, and yet have it seem that the suggestion came from the other man.

Mrs. Croy had insisted on Forrest Timkan being present. Why, I didn't know, except that I had an idea she thought I was about to perpetrate some legal skulduggery. I'd been in communication with the insurance company, and they'd sent their adjuster, a man by the name of Parker Alfman. I had a pretty shrewd idea he was also an attorney, although he was careful to masquerade as merely a representative of the company.

The weather bureau had given me the go-ahead sign. Conditions were just right for a santana. An area of unusually high barometric pressure existed in the vicinity of Winnemucca. Relatively low pressure existed off the lower part of the California coast. It was the theory of the weather bureau that these terrific winds were partially gravitational in origin, that vast masses of air collected over the interior, that the pressure tended to heat and dehydrate the air, that it started flowing along well-defined channels, gathering momentum and suffering a further loss of moisture as it swept across the arid desert region. At eight o'clock the weather man had telephoned that a terrific wind had passed through the Cajon Pass, was blowing with great intensity out through the Cucamonga district, and could be expected to hit the lower points with as much force as had been the case the night Dr. Devarest died.

You could feel the east wind in the air. People were nervous and jumpy. My skin felt dry to the touch. The membranes of my nose seemed to have been dried out in an oven. The air was unusually calm and still. Overhead, stars blazed down steadily, seeming so close that one could have knocked them out of the sky with a twenty-two rifle.

Timkan said, "I'm afraid your wind isn't going to materialize after all. Most of the time it takes a jump and misses here entirely."

"I know," I said, "but tonight the meteorological conditions are just right to give us a wind such as we had the night Dr. Devarest died."

Parker Alfman, a big-boned, arrogant past master of cynicism, looked up to where the garage door had been balanced, at a point where the lower end was just about as high as a man's head. "I don't see what you expect to prove, anyway," he said. "I've come along to watch what you're doing, but that's all. Even if the door blows down, it isn't going to mean anything to me—or to my company."

I said patiently, "On the night Dr. Devarest died, the rope was caught, just the way it is now. If the door had been fully raised, you couldn't have lowered it from the inside. The outside control is worked by a lever. A person could have stood outside the door, and closed it. Obviously, Dr. Devarest didn't go outside of the garage, close the door, then walk back in, and start to work on the motor."

"How do you know he didn't?"

"It isn't probable."

"It's probable to me."

I said, "Forty thousand bucks warps your judgment. Twelve men in a jury box would be more reasonable."

He said angrily, "That forty thousand dollars has nothing to do with it. The insurance company pays its losses. If we owe that money, we want to pay it. If we don't, we can't pay it. The law wouldn't let us."

"I know. I've heard that line so many times I know it by heart."

"It's true."

"It probably is."

"Well, what do *you* think happened?"

"Dr. Devarest raised the garage door, not all the way up, just about the height it is now, so his car could just slide under it. He knew the rope was tangled over the top of the door."

"That doesn't sound probable. How do you know he didn't fix the rope the way it is now?"

"Because the chauffeur noticed it had become tangled on that crosspiece earlier in the evening. He was going to get a stepladder and fix it—but he had a date."

"All right. The door was like this. Dr. Devarest drove in. Then what happened?"

"He had something he wanted to adjust on his motor."

"What?"

"A loose fan belt."

"The fan belt wasn't loose."

"He'd adjusted it."

"With the motor running, I suppose?"

"No. He turned the motor off while he made the repair, then he started it to see if the belt was all right. He probably was a little careless about the fumes, because *he* thought the garage door was open."

"And how did the garage door get shut?"

Just then, and before I could answer the question, the wind swooped down. A sudden, terrific first gust whipped around the house, rustling the dry fronds of palm trees into clattering activity, making a roaring sound as it swept around neighboring houses.

We waited. The door shivered and teetered.

I said, "Just watch it now."

There was a lull after the first blast of wind, then a second gust hit us. Mrs. Croy knifed the flat of her hand against her skirt, clamped the skirt firmly between her knees to hold it in place, raised her hands to her hair, fully conscious of the alluring outlines of her figure as the wind pressed her garments up against her. The illumination of the two lights in the eaves of the garage cast weird, grotesque shadows which moved in strange gyrations as the members of the party moved restlessly, bracing themselves against the onslaught of the wind.

Alfman said, "I can't give you much for your theory, Lam. It doesn't hold water. The door's teetering, but that's all."

A third blast of wind hit us. The door swayed slowly, started to move. I said, "Okay, just take a look at this."

The door suddenly slammed up, leaving the garage wide open. Alfman laughed.

I said, "The door could have been balanced just a little farther down."

"Not if he'd driven the car into the garage," Alfman said.

I pulled a lever which brought the door back down. When it was where I could reach up and grab the end, I released my grip on the lever mechanism, and moved it down a little farther. "It sticks in a place right in here."

"Sure, it does. But you can't drive a car in the garage with the door in that position."

I said, "We'll discuss that later. Let's see what the wind does first."

We didn't need to wait long for an answer. The wind was blowing more regularly now, not quite such sharp, sudden gusts, but a wall of air that had plenty of force behind it. The door teetered back and forth, then started downward. As it descended, it hit the sill with a hard jar.

Forrest Timkan said belligerently, "All right, Alfman, what's wrong with that?"

Alfman said, "I'll tell you what's wrong with it. He couldn't have driven the car through the door with the door in that position. Even if he had, he'd have heard the door hit."

"He might have been preoccupied with what he was doing."

"He'd have to have been plenty preoccupied not to have heard the bang of that door," Alfman said.

I said, "Well, let's get Dr. Devarest's car and see whether he could have driven under the door in that position."

We drove the car out. I adjusted the door in such a position that it barely cleared the top of the car. We'd made that adjustment once before. This time, regardless of Alfman's protests, I fixed it so the top of the incoming car all but grazed the lower edge.

"After all," Alfman said, "he had to get his car *in* there, you know."

I pointed to the hairline clearance between the door and the car.

"It wouldn't have touched."

"He wouldn't have tried driving in through such a narrow opening."

"You mean that he *couldn't?*"

Alfman thought that over for a moment, then said, "He wouldn't have done it."

I didn't say anything more, but ran the car on into the garage, and we stood there waiting for another gust of wind.

With the car out of the way, it looked as though it would

have been impossible to have driven the machine through that small an opening. It also looked as though the wind would have been certain to blow the door down.

The wind was blowing now in little gusts, getting ready for another big blast.

Alfman went over to his car, took out a camera with a synchronized flash gun, put in a plate holder, jerked out the slide, and said, "No human being in his right mind would try to drive a car through an opening that small."

"The car actually went through that opening."

"Sure, because it's low slung. You had to coax it along an inch at a time."

Alfman raised his camera. A white flash showed he'd taken the picture. He changed films, put in another flash bulb, walked back to the line of the street, and took another picture.

It was as he was walking toward the garage, carrying the camera in his hand, that another terrific gust of wind swirled around the houses and hit the garage.

The garage door didn't even teeter this time. It slid smoothly upward so that it was wide open.

Behind me, I heard Alfman laugh.

At my side, Bertha Cool said under her breath, "Fry me for an oyster."

Jim Timley said, "All right, folks, the show's over. I guess we can go home now."

The insurance adjuster said, "I've already started," and put his camera in the back of the car. Dr. Gelderfield leaned over to talk with Mrs. Devarest for a moment.

Timkan raised his voice and said, "Just a moment, everyone."

They stopped to look at him.

Timkan said, "Lam, have you definitely convinced yourself the counterweight on this door hasn't been tampered with?"

I said, "I looked at it just before dark. It's the same as

on the other garage doors."

Alfman got in his car and started the motor.

Dr. Gelderfield turned the wheel chair, started to take Mrs. Devarest to the house.

Timkan said, "Well, *I* didn't like the way that door acted. I'm going to take a look at that counterweight just to satisfy myself. Show me where it is, Lam."

We walked over toward the garage. Alfman switched on the headlights of his car, started to back out of the driveway, then thought better of it, parked the car and came over to see what we were doing. The wind was blowing steadily now.

I switched on the lights within the garage. Timkan looked up at the door and frowned. "There should be a counterweight," he said. "There must be."

"There's a counterweight on the underside of the door," I told him, "a thick strip of metal. You can see it hasn't been tampered with."

Timkan looked around until he found a stepladder. He got up on it and examined the door. "Yes," he said, "I guess you're right. Somehow, that door—well, it didn't do just what I thought it would do."

Alfman said breezily, "I don't want to go until the party's over. I don't want any alibis. How's the counterweight?"

Dr. Gelderfield turned the wheel chair around—waited.

"It seems okay," I told Alfman. He got back in his car.

Dr. Gelderfield, who had walked over to join us, looked at him, his forehead creased into a scowl. "I wouldn't trust that man as far as I could throw an elephant by the tail," he announced.

Bertha Cool, who had walked up to stand behind him, said, "Make it a hippopotamus as far as I'm concerned."

Dr. Gelderfield smiled at her. He'd seemed to take quite an interest in Bertha from the minute he met her. "The trouble is," he said, "so many of our corporations judge a man's value by the results that he gets. I suppose it's perfectly true the insurance corporations are willing to pay just claims, but the adjusters and district managers like to show the head office how much money they can save."

I got up on the stepladder and ran my hand over the part of the door which was concealed up near the top of the garage.

"Watch out for spiders," Bertha said. "That's a good place for a black widow spider. You'd better put on a glove, Donald Lam."

"There aren't any spider webs up here," I said, running my hand along the smooth side of the door.

Dr. Gelderfield seemed trying to impress Bertha. He said, "You can see the fact that the door is constantly in motion would—no, wait a minute. You say there aren't *any* cobwebs up there, Lam?"

I said, "No, and it strikes me as being just as significant as it does you. Wait a minute."

My fingers, sliding along the door, encountered a piece of metal. "Let's have that flashlight," I said.

Dr. Gelderfield handed it up.

I climbed up on the top rung of the stepladder. By tilting my head to one side, I could just see into the crack. A piece of metal had been clamped on to the door.

"Call the adjuster back," I said.

Dr. Gelderfield shouted at Alfman, but Alfman had his car started and was backing out of the driveway.

"What's all the excitement?" Timley asked as Dr. Gelderfield sprinted down the runway.

"A piece of metal on the door up here."

"Well, what about it?"

"It puts more weight on the back of the door, tends to make the door come back up instead of down."

"Well, what of it?"

I said, "Nothing, except it might save the insurance

137

company forty thousand bucks."

"An insurance company wouldn't do anything like that," Timley said positively.

"The *company* might not."

I heard steps, and Dr. Gelderfield came bustling back into the garage. "Now then," he said to Alfman, "we've got something else for you to take a picture of."

"What is it?" Alfman asked.

I'd been doing a little exploring while Gelderfield had gone after the adjuster. "Up here in the door," I said. "A piece of lead has been fastened on this edge."

"Nonsense," Alfman said. "You couldn't get your hand into a space that narrow. You couldn't put in a nail or a screw to save your life."

I said, "You wouldn't have to. Notice these two bolts on the underside of the door. They don't seem to serve any purpose."

"Well?"

I said, "Someone bored through the door from this side, put a strip of lead up on that part of the door, worked bolts through it, and put nuts on the bolts to hold this in place. It's been done recently."

"Since you inspected it at six o'clock?" Dr. Gelderfield asked.

I said, "I won't swear to it, because I didn't search this part of the door. I just looked at the counterweight to make certain it hadn't been tampered with."

"What are you going to do about it?" Timley asked.

"Leave it as it is. The police may be able to get finger-prints."

Dr. Gelderfield said, "I must tell my patient. Good heavens, I've left her sitting there in the wheel chair. I—"

"It's all right," Bertha said dryly. "When you were chasing after the adjuster, she got up out of the wheel chair and walked over here to see what it was all about; then she went back and became an invalid again."

Dr. Gelderfield said, "She shouldn't have done that," and dashed over to the chair.

I got down off the stepladder.

Gelderfield was bent solicitously over Mrs. Devarest, rearranging robes, asking anxious questions.

Alfman said, with every appearance of genuine anger, "This is a hell of a plant. I should have known I'd run into something like this. The whole test sounded so screwy in the first place."

"Making any insinuations?" I asked.

"You're damn right," he said. "You're trying to make the insurance company the goat in this thing. You want to say to a jury, 'Look how the insurance company tried to change the evidence.' It's a ham grandstand. You show that the test didn't work, and the widow is almost gypped out of forty thousand dollars. Then you discover where the crooked adjuster had placed a weight so it would interfere with your test. God damn you private detectives, anyway. You're all a bunch of crooks and—"

Bertha said, "Slap the bastard's face, lover."

I stepped toward him. "I don't have any idea who put that counterweight there. I'm not certain that you did. You may have. But I do know damn well I didn't."

He said sneeringly, "Baloney, you know damn well who put that weight there."

"You're a liar!" I told him.

His face flushed. He said, "Now listen, pint-size, pipe down. I hate to pick on a pipsqueak, but I've had enough dealings with you damn crooks. I—"

I saw Bertha edging toward us. I swung the open palm of my left hand against his face.

I think he was more surprised than Bertha. For a moment he stood there, his jaw sagging, then he came in with a rush.

I expected to take a licking, but I remembered some of the things Louie Hazen had taught me in the last case

I'd been on. Without even thinking what I was doing I automatically shifted to one side as Alfman lashed out with his right. His blow went over my shoulder.

It didn't seem like a fight. It seemed like just another sparring match with Louie. I held my right elbow in close to my side. As the momentum of his blow carried him toward me, I kicked my fist into his stomach with my body muscles back of it.

I felt the resistance of his taut muscles, felt them grow suddenly limp, knew he was slumping over as the solar plexus blow took effect. Once more, it was just the same as though Louie had been giving me instructions. I snapped up the right fist into a quick, jarring uppercut to catch him on the jaw as he came forward.

His teeth rattled. There was agonized surprise in his eyes, then they turned glassy.

I was conscious of a ring of startled faces around me, heard Dr. Gelderfield sputtering, "Don't look, Colette. Don't look! Let me take you away from here. You mustn't have any excitement."

Mrs. Devarest said angrily, "Take your hands off that chair. Leave me alone."

Bertha Cool screamed at me, "Go in and finish him, you damn fool. What are you standing there looking at him for?"

Alfman was weaving around on his feet. He looked at me with eyes that seemed like a couple of marbles, lashed out with his left at a point in the atmosphere a good two feet from where my chin was located. He started his right from the hip pocket in a terrific haymaker.

I stepped in on the swing and hit him in the body.

His knees buckled. He tried to throw a punch, and wobbled around off balance; then he came down hard on his face on the floor of the garage.

I stepped back out of the way. I was trembling with nervousness. I couldn't have held a match to a cigarette to save my life. I saw the awe and respect in the faces of the people that were looking at me, saw the sheer amazement on Bertha Cool's face.

I was more surprised than she was.

Bertha said, in a half whisper, "The little bastard did it!" And then, after a moment, "Pickle me for a peach."

chapter 13

BERTHA COOL slid in beside me in the front seat of the agency car. "Now what the hell was the idea of all of that?" she asked.

"Of what?"

"After you discovered that weight had been placed on the door, why didn't you take it off?"

I said, "It's good evidence leaving it on there."

"Evidence of what?"

"Evidence that someone tampered with the door."

East wind, roaring down from the mountain passes, hurtled against the car, swaying it on its springs. The long leaves of the palm trees turned so as to spill out the wind, seemed like grotesque umbrellas which had been twisted wrong side out in a storm. The dry heat evaporated perspiration almost before it formed, and the invisible particles of dust made the skin feel like parchment.

Bertha Cool said, "Look, you've got a perfect condition prevailing for a test, a desert wind blowing harder than I've seen it in a year. You may wait months before there'll be another opportunity to test that door."

I nodded.

She said, "There's a weight on the door. You can't make a fair test with the weight there. Now why in hell didn't you take it off and see what the door would do?"

"Because the door wouldn't have done anything different."

"How do you know?"

I said, "Figure it out for yourself. There's one point at

which the door catches. It swings almost in balance on the hinges. The less weight there is on the back of the door, the lower that point will be."

"Well?"

"With the weight on the back of the door, it was just about at the point where a man could drive under it. Even then, when the wind hit the door, it blew up instead of down."

"It wouldn't if it hadn't been for that weight."

"Are you certain?"

"No, but that's what I think."

I said, "It's an interesting experiment."

"Then you aren't going to try it?"

"No."

"Someone else will."

"Let them."

"Why aren't you going to?"

"Because it isn't evidence of anything. The rope was tangled up in a peculiar way. That rope is supposed to hang straight down from a lever which pulls the door down until you can reach a handle on it."

"Well?"

I said, "There's a position at which that door hangs equally balanced. With the additional weight on there, the position extends to a point where the automobile can be driven under it, but at that precise point the wind won't blow the door down and shut. It blows it up and open."

Bertha said, "What would it do without the weight on there?"

"I don't know."

"Who does?"

"Probably no one."

"Donald, you're the most exasperating little devil in the world. Sometimes, I could kill you with my bare hands. You have almost a hurricane of a desert wind, one of the hardest I can remember in a couple of years. Timkan is right. Most of them jump over this part of the valley. Only one out of every eight or ten hits here hard."

"That's right."

"You may wait for months, perhaps for years, before you'd have another chance to test your theory."

"Right."

"Well, what the devil's the idea?"

"It bothers you?"

"Of course it does."

"Then," I said, "it'll probably bother a lot of other people—including the insurance company."

Bertha blinked her hard little eyes as she tried to digest the full import of that statement. "You mean you're trying to worry the insurance company?"

"That's one of the things."

She thought that over for a while, and then said, "You're a brainy little cuss. You're going to make the insurance company compromise on that case. You've got them worried about that door. When you said you didn't want it touched, but wanted it left exactly as it was so the police could look it over and try to get fingerprints off that weight, you *really* worried them."

"That won't hurt them any."

She said, "I see now what you're driving at. They'll think that in place of trying to sell the jury on the test, you're going to advance your theory, claim that it's self-evident it would have worked if it hadn't been for the counterweight on the door, then show the counterweight, and dump the thing into the lap of the insurance company. The company can't order up another east wind to prove you're wrong."

I didn't say anything.

"You're playing some sort of a deep game," she said irritably, "and when you do that, you make me mad. You never would take me into your confidence. Where the hell are you going now?" she interpolated as I pulled in to the curb.

"I'm telephoning from this drugstore to get a taxicab to take you home."

She flared into temper. "Damn your pint-sized soul."

I locked the ignition on the agency car, put the key in my pocket.

"What are you doing that for?"

"So you won't get independent, drive the car away, and leave me afoot. A taxi should be here in a few minutes."

I went into the drugstore and telephoned for a cab. When I came back, Bertha was sitting behind the wheel, her jaw thrust out defiantly. "I won't budge from this car," she announced, "until you've told me what it's all about."

"If I tell you, will you co-operate?"

"Why, certainly."

"Well," I said, "it's this way. Dr. Devarest had been given a package of jewels to deliver to his grandmother, but the big bad wolf thought that he could pretend to be Dr. Devarest's grandmother and so get the jewels. He—"

"Shut up!"

I kept quiet.

Bertha sat rigidly erect, exuding indignation for a while, then she turned to say something; but the words died on her lips as her eyes grew suddenly solicitous. "What's that on your cheek?" she asked.

"Where?"

Her fingers touched it. It was sore.

Bertha said, "It's a bruise. It's where that chap hit you."

"He didn't hit me."

"I think it was his arm or his shoulder. You certainly doubled him up. My God, Donald, you could have knocked me over with a feather. Imagine seeing you *win* a fight. And when you pick on someone, you certainly do pick out the big ones."

"Louie always claimed the bigger they were, the slower they were, and the easier it was to put them out."

"Well, you certainly put him out. Why the hell is it that a good fight appeals to a woman? I don't mean the fight so much, but when she sees a man win the fight, she goes nuts over him."

"Are you nuts over me?"

"You little bastard, I could slap your teeth down your throat. Shut up! Of course, I'm not nuts over you. I never went nuts over any man. I'm talking about that Croy woman."

"What about her?"

"You should have seen her eyes when she was looking at you, the expression on her face, everything about her."

A taxi swung around the corner. The headlights swung in close to the curb. "Here's your transportation," I told Bertha.

"I'm not getting out until you tell me what it's all about and what you're going to do."

"You want to go fishing tomorrow?" I asked.

She hesitated a moment, then said, "What's that got to do with it?"

"Under our contract with Mrs. Devarest, we get a slice of forty thousand dollars if we can make the insurance company kick through."

"Well, what about it?"

I said, "Our chances of making it kick through are ten times better if I play a lone hand."

"You play too many lone hands."

I said, "I don't know whether it's ever occurred to you, but if I violate a law, it's my own responsibility. If I tell you I'm going to violate a law, and you expect to participate in the money I get as a result of that law violation, you're a conspirator. You're—"

She was halfway out of the car. "I suppose that's just a damn bluff," she said, "but it's going to work. Go ahead,

145

lover, and get that wad of dough. Bertha's going fishing."

She paused, halfway to the taxi, came back to say in a low voice, "Be careful, Donald. You don't know where to stop. You get started on something and you forget there's any limit on the betting."

"You want results, don't you?"

"I want you to stay out of state prison long enough to make me some money—damn you."

The taxi driver held the door open. Bertha flounced in indignantly. I didn't wait for the cab to pull away, but jabbed the key in the ignition lock and started the car back toward Dr. Devarest's house. I parked it a block down the street, walked along the sidewalk, saw there were lights on in the house, but no one in the driveway. The light over the garage doors had been turned off, and the doors were all closed. There was a light in the windows of the chauffeur's quarters over the garage, not anything particularly noticeable, just the diffused faint illumination such as would come through Venetian blinds.

I skirted the house, walking along the grassy part of the driveway to the garage, climbed the stairs, and tapped on the door. Rufus Bayley opened the door a crack, saw who it was, and said, "Come on in."

I went in and the hot, dry wind came sweeping in after me. I forced the door closed, walked over, and sat down. I felt as though there were a layer of sandpaper between my skin and my clothes.

"Did you have an opportunity to go through the house okay?"

"Did I! Buddy, you're a wonder. I went through the joint from soup to nuts. What I mean is, starting that fight was a swell idea. I even had a chance to go through the safe again."

"How did you get the combination to the safe?"

He grinned. "There's been a lot of talk about it and about how the doctor had it written down in code in his book. You don't think I'm going to let anything like that slip past, do you?"

"What did you find?"

"The sparklers."

"Where?"

"In Jim Timley's room just like you said, done up in a brown paper package."

"Did you bring the package?"

"Don't be silly. We'd have both had a one-way ticket to San Quentin if I'd done that. You can gamble he'll take a look for that package the last thing before he goes to bed tonight. If he finds it's missing, he'll think back over what happened tonight, and know damn well there was only one time when anyone could have frisked the place. That was a swell idea of yours getting them all out front, but it works both ways. Everyone had an alibi except little old me. I don't crave to—"

"So what did you do about the package?"

"I just did a swell job of it," he said, flashing his teeth again. "I took the sparklers out. They were in books— slickest thing you ever saw. The inside of the pages had been cut out on the books, and the jewels put inside. Well, I just untied the package, took out the jewels, stuck 'em in my pocket, then carefully wrapped the books up just the way they had been. I even tied the string in the same sort of a knot that had been on it when I first found it. It was a damn granny—a woman's knot."

"What were the books? Do you remember?"

"Why, just books."

"You don't remember what the names of them were, who wrote them, what they were about?"

He frowned. "What's that got to do with it?"

"It might be a clue that would help."

"Help what? Once you get the sparklers, what do you care about the clues?"

"It might give me a better picture of what happened."

"Hell, you know what happened. This Nollie Starr and Jim Timley played it together. She lifted the swag, kept it out of the house while the police were frisking the joint, and then when the smoke blew over, Timley went down and got 'em back. He either doesn't trust her to keep them, or she refused to have the evidence on her—and you can't blame her any for that."

"Where are they?"

He fished his hand down in his side pocket, carelessly pulled out a glittering assortment of gems, and dumped them on the table, groping around casually as though he had had a pocketful of beans, and wanted to make certain none of the beans escaped him. He found a couple of stragglers, put them on the table with the others, and said, "That's all."

Light falling on the pile on the table was reflected in coruscations of scintillating brilliance: green, shimmery shafts from emeralds; hard, sparkling off-shoots of light from the facets of diamonds.

Bayley looked at the pile and said, wistfully, "Cripes, I wish I'd dared to give you a double-cross on that stuff. That really *is* something."

"Is that all of it?" I asked.

"Uh huh."

"Turn your pocket wrong side out."

He scowled at me and said, "Listen, buddy, when I tell you that's all, I mean that's all. I don't double-cross my pals. You and I are in this thing together, old kid. See? I did a stretch once, but it cured me. I'm going straight. I—"

"Turn out your pocket then."

"Say, who do you think you're talking to?"

"You."

"Well, think again."

I said, "You're giving yourself away. If you'd pulled the lining of your pocket inside out, and *then* got mad, it

148

would have impressed me. As it is, you're just making things worse."

"Oh, hell," he said, and shot his hand down into his pocket, fumbled around for a moment, catching the lining of the coat, then jerked it inside out. "Now, are you satisfied?" he asked.

I moved over closer.

"Go ahead, buddy, take a look for yourself," he said, swinging around so I could see the lining of his pocket.

His left hand was held out away from his side, the fingers spread wide apart, the back toward me. I grabbed it, and jerked the fingers back so that the skin was pulled tight across the palms.

Two big diamond rings fell to the floor.

"Pick them up and put them on the table," I said.

His thick lips pushed together to blot out the grin. He said, "You can only crowd me so far, buddy."

"Pick up the rings and put them on the table with the other junk."

He kept staring at me, hot rage in his eyes. "Look," he said, "you're pretty shifty. I saw the way you handled your mitts, but you can't—"

"Put those rings on the table," I told him, "and then sit down. We'll talk things over."

He hesitated for a long two or three seconds; then bent over and picked up the rings. When he straightened, he was smiling once more, the genial smile of a good-natured giant.

"What the hell, buddy? I wasn't really trying to hold out on you, just those two sparklers that I wanted to play with a little bit. They're beauties. Sit down over there and give me the dope. What's next?"

I walked over to the table and put the jewelry into my coat pocket before I said anything. The way his eyes were watching me, I knew how a canary feels when the door of the cage pops open and the family cat crawls up on the table.

I inventoried the stuff as I put it in my pocket. "One diamond and emerald bracelet, one ruby pendant, one diamond brooch, four diamond solitaire rings, one emerald ring with a diamond on each side, one diamond necklace—you're sure that's all of it, Bayley?"

"Word of honor," he said.

I sat down in the chair, settled back with the best imitation of careless ease I could give, and lit a cigarette.

He started to sit down by the window, then changed his mind and walked over so he was sitting between me and the door. The grin on his face was fixed now, just a frozen leer that he tried in vain to change into a smile. His eyes were watching my every move.

I said, "Who put the extra weight on the garage door, Bayley?"

"I don't know."

"Don't you think you'd better find out?"

"Why?"

"Oh, nothing. I just thought it might be a good idea."

Bayley said, "Listen, buddy. Don't get me wrong. You're where you can push me around right now, but you can only push me so hard, and you can only push me so far. One of these days I'll be the boss here."

I laughed at him, and my laughter intensified the glint of hatred in his eyes. "What's funny about that?" he demanded.

"You are."

"Why me?"

"Overlooking what's happening right under your nose."

"All right, wise guy, what's happening under my nose?"

"Corbin Harmley."

It took a minute for the impact of the remark to smack home in his brain. Then, when the full import of what I had said registered with him, I saw the anger in his eyes give place to startled apprehension. His self-assurance dropped from him, leaving him the overgrown boy, a big hunk of masculine immaturity, sitting there staring at me with comprehension of what was happening knocking the props out from under his self-esteem.

It was almost thirty seconds before he said, with a slow deliberation which gave emphasis to his words, "By—God."

I followed up. "You may have thought Mrs. Devarest was pretty strong for you, and that you could strut all over the place, posing in front of her to let her see how big and strong you were. What you overlooked was the fact that Harmley has all you've got and a lot more. He has an education, culture, and a profile. Mrs. Devarest is flattered and interested."

Bayley said with feeling, "Why, the dirty skunk! If he tries any of that— I'll— I'll—"

"Yes, go on, Bayley. What will you do?"

He let his head sway sullenly from side to side in a surly gesture. "No, you don't," he said. "You don't trap me."

I watched him shifting uneasily in the chair. "I was just wondering," I said.

"Well, go ahead and wonder."

"What makes you think Mrs. Devarest would have stood up in front of a minister with you? Usually widows like to fluff their feathers for a while just to see if they have wings and can really fly."

He said, "Nuts, I can get any dame I really want to."

"That takes in a lot of territory."

His thick lips broke into a sneer. "Doesn't it?" he asked, and then after a moment added, "I know what I'm talking about. You try to hand a woman a line, and make her, and sometimes you get to first base, and then get thrown out trying to steal second. But get a woman interested in you, and then just don't do a damn thing about it, and you got her worried. After a while, she starts making little advances. You don't pay any attention to them. Then she comes all the way. And once a woman has gone all the way with me, I can make her do anything. She's mine from then on."

I said, "I think Harmley will ask her to marry him tonight."

I saw his eyes widen as he thought that over. It was my chance. I got up and walked on past him out of the door.

chapter 14

THE CLERK in the probate department looked at me dubiously. "What did you say your name was?"

"Lam—Donald Lam."

"You're not a lawyer?"

"No."

"What is your occupation, Mr. Lam?"

I gave her one of my cards. She studied it and seemed dubious about what to do with it, then she said, "Just what is it you want?"

I said, "I'd like a list of cases which are in probate where a man died leaving a good-sized estate, but no business associates."

"I don't think I understand. We don't keep files listed in a way to get that information."

I said, "A man such as a doctor practicing medicine by himself, being fairly well-to-do, and leaving quite a chunk of property."

She shook her head. "We can't handle things that way. You'll have to tell me what specific estate you want to find out about."

I went into the telephone booth, called the secretary of the medical association, and asked him to read me obituary notices of the most prominent and successful doctors who had died during the past year. I got half a dozen names, among them that of Dr. Devarest. Then I went back to the girl at the desk. Within ten minutes I had the files of half a dozen estates.

I went to work on the telephone, in the booth at the corner of the probate clerk's office.

With the first woman, I drew a blank. With the second, I started the same line. "Excuse me please, but I'm telephoning from the probate clerk's office at the courthouse. I want to find out something about your husband's estate."

"Yes. What was it you wanted to know?"

"During your husband's lifetime, did he have some business dealings with a chap in the early thirties who has dark, wavy hair, a long, straight nose, a clean-cut profile, a habit of holding his chin high, who has nice eyes, that are capable of expressing sympathy, humor, and—"

"Why, yes," she interrupted. "Mr. Harmley."

"Did that deal involve some South American properties?"

"No, it didn't. The only business connection my husband had with him was to lend him money. He lent him a small sum, and Mr. Harmley was very grateful."

"Two hundred and fifty dollars?"

"Yes."

"Mr. Harmley returned from South America and repaid the money?"

She said, "He arrived in town, as it happened, the day my husband died. He read the notice in the paper, and got in touch with me, sending me a little note of condolence and a check for the two hundred and fifty dollars together with six months' interest. He said he hoped it would help to defray the expenses."

"And your husband didn't have any interest in the oil properties?"

"My *husband* didn't, no."

There was just a faint accent on the word *husband*.

"You have acquired some interest yourself?"

"I don't see what that has to do with it. Who is this talking, please, and what did you want to know?"

I said patiently, "Madam, we're simply trying to find

out whether those oil securities were your own investment, or were acquired by your husband as the result of a previous loan. In the latter event, it makes a difference about the inventory and the inheritance tax."

"Oh," she said, mollified. "No. My husband had nothing to do with them. They're purely my own individual property."

"Thank you," I said and hung up.

I climbed the three flights of stairs at 681 East Bendon Street. It was about eleven-thirty in the morning. The odds were greatly in my favor that neither Dorothy Grail nor Nollie Starr would be in, but I went through the motions of knocking on the door. No one answered. The lock was a cinch. Probably the apartment had maid service once a week, and the lock was a type which a simple passkey would operate.

I closed the door behind me. The spring lock clicked into place. I went to work methodically, starting first with the living-room, and particularly interesting myself in the books.

There were plenty of books. About ninety per cent of them were detective stories by the most popular authors, picked with shrewd judgment. Evidently this was where Dr. Devarest disposed of his surplus mystery books.

There was a wall bed. I swung it out to inspect the counterpane, and the wrinkles in the pillowslips. It looked as though the bed was just about due for a change. The closet in the space surrounding the wall bed was fairly well filled with a woman's clothes. I looked them over and decided they were Dorothy Grail's clothes. She evidently used this bed. Nollie Starr then would use the bedroom.

I gently pushed open the bedroom door, stepped inside. I noticed that the shades were drawn. The possibility that Nollie Starr, early morning tennis enthusiast, cyclist and pep exponent, would lower the shades and sleep until almost noon hadn't occurred to me. When the idea did strike me, I turned to the bed apprehensively.

The woman lay stretched out on the counterpane, her left hand thrown upward over her eyes, her hair streaming out to fall in confusion against the counterpane. She was wearing a very thin peach-colored nightgown which was pulled up from shapely legs.

I stood for a moment, motionless.

Slowly, I began tiptoeing toward the door, careful lest I should disturb the late sleeper. I glanced over my shoulder to see if some restless motion, some long, tremulous sigh would presage wakefulness.

There was no motion.

I was almost at the door when the white silence of the figure impressed me more than the dangerous predicament in which I found myself. There was just enough light to show a peculiar color to the skin.

I walked back to touch the bare flesh of the ankle. The skin was warm to the touch, but I knew it was inanimate as soon as my fingers felt of it. I picked up the left arm— a pink cord had been wound tightly around the neck. In the back of this cord the handle of a potato masher had been inserted and twisted, drawing the cord fiendishly tight.

I untwisted the cord, loosened it from where it had bitten into the swollen flesh. I felt the pulse, leaned over to listen for a heartbeat.

There was perhaps one chance in ten thousand that a Pulmotor could do some good. I went to the telephone, dialed the emergency number, and explained to the operator what I wanted.

The gems which had been taken from Dr. Devarest's safe were in a belt next to my skin. The police would naturally want to know how I happened to get in. They'd want to know what I had intended to do when I went there. They'd search me. When they searched me, they'd find the gems. The police mind would put two and two together, and it would make a quick four. Nollie Starr had either taken the gems from the safe, or had taken them from Dr. Devarest. I had gone to recover them. Nollie Starr had been asleep in the bedroom. She'd wakened and started to scream. I'd silenced her—perhaps not intending to kill her, but had held the cord a little too tight and a little too long. The Pulmotor squad was on its way. There was nothing I could gain by staying.

I wiped the telephone with my handkerchief, polished off the doorknobs, and walked boldly out into the hall.

A woman of about forty-five, heavy set, muscular, and capable, was walking toward me, carrying a vacuum cleaner. She regarded me casually at first, then with sudden interest.

I walked down the stairs to the street. A siren was screaming for the right of way at the intersection. I stood gawking just as the rest of the pedestrians were doing, watching men pull out a Pulmotor, and dash across the sidewalk to the entrance of the building.

Most of the crowd dispersed, but a few remained to stare at the building entrance, apparently expecting the walls of the masonry to give some answer to their morbid curiosity.

I walked over to where I had parked the agency car, climbed in, and drove down to the parking lot where we kept the bus. The attendant gave me a nod. I made my greeting casual and went up to the office.

Elsie Brand looked up from her typing as I opened the door.

"How's the high-priced secretary getting along?" I asked.

"Thanks to you," she said, "the high-priced secretary is doing very nicely."

"Bertha in?"

Elsie Brand swung away from her typewriter, lowered

her voice. "She's in and on the warpath."

"What about?"

"You."

"What have I done now?"

"Something with the police. You're in hot water."

"Know what it's about?"

"You tried to hold out something on Lieutenant Lisman, and he's putting Bertha on the pan."

"Hold out on him!" I exclaimed. "I dropped a bouquet in his lap when I let him find that Starr girl."

"It's a bouquet all right," she said, smiling. "But he doesn't like the smell of it."

"Well, to hell with him. I—"

The door of the private office burst open explosively. Bertha Cool stood glaring at me.

"*Now*, what the hell are you doing?" she asked.

"Talking."

"Raising Elsie's wages again, I suppose."

I said, "That might be a good idea. The cost of living is going up."

"Some day I'm going to skin you alive, you damn little runt."

"What have I been doing now?" I asked.

"Plenty. Come in here."

"I'll be in as soon as I've finished my conversation with Elsie."

Bertha's face got white with rage. "You come in here or I'll—I'll—"

"Do what?" I asked quietly.

Bertha Cool slammed the door.

Elsie Brand said, "She'll have a fit, Donald. I never saw her that mad before."

I said, "I think she's getting more emotional now that she's taken off weight."

"Aren't you afraid of her?"

"Why should I be?"

"I don't know. She's ruthless. When she gets it in for anyone, she never gets over it."

"Do you think she's getting it in for you?" I asked.

"She didn't like the way you raised my wages."

"But you're getting the raise all right?"

"Yes."

"That's good. See that you keep on getting it. Well, I'll go and relieve the old girl's blood pressure."

I crossed the office and opened the door. Bertha was sitting back of her big desk, her lips clamped tight, her eyes cold and sparkling.

"Shut the door," she said.

The rapid beat of Elsie Brand's fingers on the keyboard of the typewriter sent a machine-gun clatter pouring through the doorway before the latch clicked it shut.

"All right, what's the trouble?"

"What did you mean, holding out on Lieutenant Lisman?"

"I didn't hold out on him."

"He thinks you did."

"I told him where the Starr girl could be found."

"Yes. He fell for that. It was a nice sop."

"What do you mean, a sop?"

"You're a smart little bastard, aren't you?"

"Never mind the affection. What are you getting at?"

"Why didn't you tell Lisman about that chauffeur being a convict?"

"He didn't ask me."

"No. But you used him to get the dope—made him a cat's-paw."

"I asked him a question. He gave me the information. What's wrong with that?"

"You know what's wrong with it. You slipped one over on him."

"He knows now?"

"Of course, he knows now."

I sat on the edge of Bertha Cool's desk and lit a cigarette. "That doesn't look so good."

"I'll tell the world it doesn't look so good. He thinks the agency is refusing to co-operate with him. He's sore, and I mean *really* sore."

"That isn't bothering me," I said. "The question is, what's he doing with Rufus Bayley?"

She said, "He's got Rufus Bayley down at headquarters, and he's doing plenty to him."

I spilled ashes off the end of my cigarette on Bertha's desk. She indignantly shoved an ash tray across and said, "Watch what you're doing."

I left my hat on the corner of the desk, said, "Hold everything for a minute. I left the car parked in front of a fire hydrant. There was no other place."

She said, "You sit right there, and tell me what you're trying to put across with Lisman. I've told you repeatedly not to leave the car in front of the fire plug. It will serve you right to pay a fine."

"It's the agency car," I said.

"Well, what of it?"

I said, "The fine would go on the expense account—now that I'm a partner."

She pushed back her chair, started to get up, then settled back. "Get down and get that car moved! Don't stick around here all day. Get going!"

I walked out of the door, crossed the office, and paused by Elsie Brand's desk.

She looked up. I said, "Elsie, I'm in a jam. What can you do about it?"

"What's the matter?"

I said, "I've got Mrs. Devarest's jewelry on me. I wanted a chance to return it when I wanted and in the way I wanted. I had the cards turn against me. I'm hot as a stove lid."

"Want me to take the jewelry?"

159

"It'd be dangerous."

"Okay, give."

I said, "There's another way out."

"What?"

"I still may have a chance to put that jewelry where I want it."

"Go ahead."

"I've got to have a hideout, a place where they won't look for me."

She was opening her purse, almost before I'd finished speaking. "Here's the key," she said, "and for God's sake, Donald, don't judge me by that apartment. I got up late this morning. The bed isn't made—the place is a sight. I just jumped into my shoes and walked out."

"Okay, be seeing you."

"Does Bertha know?"

"No one knows. Bertha thinks I've gone down to move the agency car."

Elsie Brand closed her purse matter-of-factly, swung back to the keyboard, and exploded the typewriter into noise.

I went down to the parking lot, picked up the agency car, drove it across the street, parked it in front of a fire plug where the police would be sure to tag it, hopped aboard a streetcar, rode for half a dozen blocks, took a taxi to Elsie's Brand's apartment house, used her key, and went in.

There were dirty dishes on the sink. The bed was just the way it had been thrown back when the alarm went off. Silk pajamas were thrown across the back of a chair. There was a line stretched across the bathroom over the tub, and a couple of pairs of stockings and some silk panties were drying on the line.

I pulled the covers back up on the bed, and started prowling the apartment, looking for something to read. I found a book, read, then turned on the radio. With

160

the radio on, I dozed off to a warm lethargy of half sleep.

The mention of my own name caused me to snap wide awake, listening to the voice of the news broadcaster, speaking with a rapid-fire, crisp delivery. "—Donald Lam, a private detective, is being hunted by police in connection with the theft of some twenty thousand dollars in jewelry belonging to Mrs. Colette Devarest. Rufus Bayley, an ex-convict, stated to Lieutenant Lisman that Lam had approached him with a scheme. According to Bayley, Lam actually found the body of Dr. Devarest nearly an hour before, and, accompanied by the doctor's niece, led the way to the garage to investigate the sound of a running motor. On his first discovery of the body, Lam had found the jewel cases in the glove compartment of Dr. Devarest's car, so the chauffeur swore to police. According to Bayley's statement, Lam had appropriated the gems, switched on the ignition again, started the motor, and more than an hour later instituted the investigation which led to a discovery of the physician's body. Bayley insists Lam approached him with a scheme to dispose of the gems. Bayley, who says he is now going straight, claims to have refused, and swears he was on his way to police headquarters when detectives picked him up. Because the autopsy indicates that Dr. Devarest may have been unconscious for an hour before his body was found, but had probably not been dead that long, police point out that the action of the private investigator in turning on the engine, after once shutting it off, may have amounted to at least a technical murder. . . ."

I shut off the radio, reached for the telephone, then changed my mind. There was a switchboard operator on duty at the desk. If she saw a light flash on in Elsie Brand's apartment during the hours Elsie was at work, she might get suspicious and listen in on the conversation.

Elsie hadn't called me to report—probably for that same reason.

chapter 15

ELSIE CAME IN about five-thirty. I saw her look swiftly up and down the corridor as she pulled the door shut.

She took off her hat, tossed her purse and hat on the table, looked around the apartment, and said, "God, what a mess!"

"What happened at the office?"

"A little of everything, Donald, I'd rather have cut off a right hand than have let you see my apartment with its hair down this way."

"It's all right. What happened? Who came to the office?"

"Everybody. Lieutenant Lisman for a starter."

"What did he want?"

She moved out into the kitchen and made a face at the sinkful of dirty dishes. "You."

"What did Bertha tell him?"

"That you'd gone down to move the agency car, that you'd left it in front of a fire plug."

"How long after I left the office did Lisman come in?"

"Probably not over ten minutes."

"What did Lisman do?"

Elsie turned on the hot water in the sink, turned to say something to me, and caught sight of the pajamas on the back of the chair. She left the water running in the sink, grabbed up the pajamas, hung them in the closet, started back toward the sink, saw the socks and panties on the line in the bathroom, made a dive for the door, then stopped, and burst out laughing. "Well, at least you won't have any illusions left."

"What did Lisman do?" I asked.

"He called Bertha a clumsy liar, then went down and found the agency car actually parked in front of a fire plug. That bothered him. Your hat was in the office. He thought perhaps something had happened to you after you'd left the office and before you got to the car."

"He didn't talk with the attendant on the parking lot, did he?"

"I don't know."

"Did he question you?"

"I'll say."

"What did you tell him?"

"That you'd been in and gone out."

"Did he ask if I'd talked with you?"

"Certainly."

"What did you tell him?"

"Told him you were telling me a story."

I grinned. "What was the story?"

She said, "Aren't men funny? That was exactly what Lieutenant Lisman wanted to know."

"What did you tell him?"

"I told him I didn't know him that well."

"What did he say?"

"Oh, I've forgotten the exact words, but it changed the subject of conversation very nicely. He told me an officer can really show a girl a swell time because people always put themselves out to be nice to a police officer."

"What did you say to that?"

"I asked him if the girls were supposed to do that, too."

"What did he say?"

She spilled soap powder into the dishpan, churned it up into a creamy froth, flashed me a glance over her right shoulder, and said, "What do you *think*? Are you going to wipe dishes for me?"

"Uh huh."

"The towel's over on the hanger behind the stove. I'd never make anyone a good wife. I hate housework."

"So do I."

"A man's supposed to hate it. It's a sign of something when a woman does."

"But you do?"

"Definitely. That's why I'm working."

She plunged dishes into the hot suds, dabbed at them with the dish mop, fished out a plate, and handed it to me.

"Don't you rinse them?" I asked.

She said, "I don't."

"What's this on there?"

"That is egg yolk," she said. "It's hardened, coagulated, oxidized, or whatever the hell you want to call it. Here, give it back to me. Let's let the thing soak for half an hour. How about a drink?"

I said, "It's illuminating to get the low-down on a girl's character. When I first came to the office, you wouldn't even look up from your keyboard when I came in. You were as aloof as a politician the first year after election. I thought you were a self-contained woman who simply adored prowling around your apartment with a dust cloth wrapped around your forefinger, dabbing at little specks of dirt, and burnishing everything until it shone."

She said, "I told you I hate housework, and I never mix business with pleasure."

"Meaning me?"

"Meaning you."

"Got anything to drink in the place?"

"I think there's a little Scotch left."

"How about going down and buying some?"

"We can beat that. There's a liquor store in the block. They'll send it up."

I said, "I've got some money."

She went to the telephone, picked up the receiver, and said, "Hello, Doris. How's everything tonight? . . . Oh, so-so. . . . Beastly. . . . I'll say—how about getting me the liquor store? . . . Okay, I will."

She hung onto the line for a moment, then said, "Hello, this is Elsie Brand. How are you tonight? . . . I'm swell. . . . Uh huh—how's for a bottle of House of Lords and a bottle of cocktails?" She placed her hand over the transmitter, turned to me, and asked, "Martinis or Manhattans?"

"Martinis."

She said into the telephone, "A bottle of House of Lords, a club dry Martini. Put in three bottles of White Rock, and be sure it's cold, will you, Bert? That's a good egg. Send Eddie right up with them—will you? Okay, thanks."

She hung up the telephone, turned and surveyed the bed. "Where are *you* going to sleep?" she asked.

I said, "That's an interesting question. Where *am* I going to sleep?"

"That's no reason I shouldn't make up the bed. Give me a hand with the sheet on that side. Not too hard. You're pulling it loose at the bottom. Now the blanket. Where's the jewelry?"

"In your top bureau drawer."

"How nice!"

"Isn't it?"

"Think the police will pay me a visit?"

"I doubt it. The car in front of the fire plug will give them something to think about."

She sat down. "Donald, is there anything else? Is it just over that jewelry? I had an idea, from the way police activity picked up around the office this afternoon, there might have been something else."

"There is."

"How about telling me?"

"There's so darn much I wouldn't know where to begin."

"Is that a stall?"

"Uh huh."

"Why? Don't you want me to know?"

"It's better if you didn't."

"Why?"

"Because you're just a stenographer who knows nothing of what goes on in the private offices. You thought Lisman wanted me just as clients want me. You came home and found me in your apartment. I kidded you along and told you I'd dropped in just a few minutes before you got here, that I wanted to talk to you. I told you I'd buy a drink. You kept asking me how I'd got in, and I'd insisted I'd found the door open. You thought perhaps I'd had a pass-key, but I bought you a drink and you asked me about the police. I told you that I'd seen Lieutenant Lisman and had just left his office, that the reason I came up here was because I wanted to dictate some letters that could go out early in the morning, that as soon as I dictated the letters, I was on my way."

She thought that over and said, "I *might* make that stick." A knock sounded on the door. She said, "Here's the booze, Donald. Give me some money."

I handed her a ten-dollar bill. She opened the door about eighteen inches, held her foot against it to keep it from opening any farther, shoved out the ten-dollar bill, and said, "Hello, Eddie. How much?"

He handed her two paper bags, said, "Six twenty, including the tax." I heard the rustle of currency, the clink of coins, and then he said, "Thanks a lot, Miss Brand."

Elsie closed the door, and I took the two paper bags out to the kitchen.

Elsie got ice cubes out of the refrigerator, said, "I suppose I'm going to be a martyr and cook dinner."

"Who's going to be a martyr?"

She laughed and said, "I got the shoe on the wrong foot. You are."

"We could open a can of beans."

"That'd be swell," Elsie said. "Just beans is all we need— if it suits you all right."

"It suits me."

She got a cocktail shaker and said, "Hold out your glass."

I held out my glass. We sipped the cocktail, then had another. She said, "Well, I'll go down and get the can of beans. We might have an avocado salad to go with it."

"Swell."

"And maybe brown bread? They have it canned. All you need to do is put it in boiling water for about twenty minutes. It melts in your mouth."

"Suits me." I took out my wallet, gave her another ten dollars.

"Are we eating on Bertha Cool?" she asked.

"Yes."

"That's fine. I know where there's a place that specializes in homemade chocolate pies. They're about an inch and a half thick, and just a creamy chocolate. We could get a half a chocolate pie and—"

"Sold," I told her.

She put on her hat and was humming a little tune as she looked at herself in the mirror.

"How are you coming with the Devarest insurance business?"

"Pretty good."

She said, "That isn't what Bertha Cool told me. Bertha said you'd pulled a boner."

I laughed.

"Didn't you?"

"It depends on how you look at it."

"Donald Lam, did you put that weight on the door so it acted that way?"

"No."

"Who did?"

"Someone who wanted my experiment to be a success."

"I don't get you."

I said, "The door hinges on a pivot. There is, however, one critical place at which the door will be perfectly balanced. A strong gust of wind would upset that balance and blow it open or shut. That point of balance normally is when the door is only about four feet off the ground. Dr. Devarest couldn't have driven his car in. Someone tampered with the point of balance so it would be just high enough so that a car could squeeze under it. The person who did that hoped the wind would close the garage door from that point. It was a bum guess."

"And you knew that when the tests were being made?"

"I suspected it."

She said, "I guess Bertha's right. You're a funny cuss. You certainly play them close to your chest. Well, I'm going out and get our dinner. Anything else you want?"

"No, that's plenty."

She went out, was gone twenty minutes, came back with two market bags full of packages.

"Gosh, Donald, things looked so good down in the store. Do you know what I got?"

"No."

She said, "We're going to have the beans all right, and the brown bread, and the salad."

"And the chocolate pie?" I asked.

"And the chocolate pie, but in addition to that, I got a swell porterhouse steak about two inches thick, and some ale—"

"Did you get the ale?"

"Uh huh, and some potato chips and a can of asparagus and a loaf of sourdough French bread. We'll cut that right down the middle and put it in the broiler alongside the steak until it—"

"You'd better get started," I told her.

"I am getting started."

She went out in the little kitchenette and dumped her bundles down on the drainboard of the sink.

"What can I do?" I asked.

"Not a thing. It's too cramped in here for two people to work. I'll have things going in just a jiffy."

I could hear her bustling around in the kitchen, and after a few minutes, the smell of broiling steak caressed my palate.

"How about another cocktail?" Elsie Brand called from

the kitchenette.

"How long before we eat?"

"About five minutes. Tell you what let's do, Donald. Let's have a quick cocktail, and then you can set the table."

We had our cocktail. Elsie got up and started for the kitchen. The telephone rang. She called over her shoulder, "Get that, will you, Donald?"

"I'd better not."

"That's right. I'll see who it is. You take a look at the steak."

She picked up the telephone, said, "Hello. . . . Yes. . . . Who? . . . Oh, my God!"

She slammed the telephone receiver back, and said to me, "That's the desk. They just telephoned that Bertha Cool was on her way up here."

I stood perfectly still for a moment.

Elsie Brand said, in a panic, "No, you don't, Donald. Don't you see? She'll remember about my raise, and then when she comes and finds me cooking dinner for you in my apartment. Get in that closet, close the door, and stay there."

I still hesitated.

"You can't put *me* on a spot, Donald. Hurry up. Here she is now."

Knuckles tapped heavily on the door.

I slipped in the closet. Elsie Brand closed the door, and I heard her call, "Who is it?"

Bertha said, "It's me."

I heard the sound of the outer door being unlocked and opened; then Bertha Cool, giving an audible sniff and saying, "Just cooking dinner?"

"Just broiling a steak."

"Go right ahead, dearie. I'll come out in the kitchen and talk with you."

"No, you won't," Elsie said, laughing. "That kitchen is hardly big enough to hold me. The steak's just at the

crucial moment. You sit down right here and have a cigarette. I'll shut off the fire. Perhaps things will wait, or—
or—" Her voice trailed off into dubious, uncordial silence.

Bertha Cool said, "Go right ahead. That cooking smells
good. I'm hungry."

"Or I was going to suggest that if you hadn't had
dinner—"

"Well, go ahead and suggest it. What the hell's stopping
you?"

Elsie laughed and said, "There's just a little more cocktail."

"It's nice that you can *afford* cocktails whenever you
want them," Bertha said pointedly. "Where is it?"

"I'll get it."

There was silence for a moment, then the sound of the
oven door opening, and the odor of broiled steak was suddenly intensified. I heard Bertha moving around, then
her voice saying, "You certainly got a golden brown on
that French bread. No, don't put any butter on mine.
Well—well, after all, I suppose this is really a special occasion and a diet shouldn't be taken too seriously."

Elsie said, "Just a moment. I'll get some things on the
table."

"Where are the dishes? I'll help."

"You wouldn't know where things are, Mrs. Cool. Just
sit down and relax."

I heard Elsie Brand's quick steps coming and going.
She was all but running. I could hear plates clatter on the
table.

Bertha said, "Fry me for an oyster!"

"What's the matter?" Elsie Brand asked.

"A steak that size when you're eating alone."

Elsie Brand said quickly, "There's not much fun in
cooking when you're all by yourself, so I usually get a big
steak, have it hot the first night, have cold steak the second
night, and make hash the third night."

Bertha sniffed at that. I guess she didn't like cold steak.

"Don't ever eat too much," Bertha said. "I used to let myself go, and I got altogether too fat. That illness was the best thing that ever happened to me. I feel ever so much better now."

"Yes, you look better. Was there something you wanted —something particular you had in mind?"

Bertha said, "Where's Donald?"

"Why, when he left the office—you know he said something about his car in front of the fire plug, and then—"

"He hasn't been here?"

"Why, Mrs. Cool, what on earth would he want to come here for?"

"Well, he's some place, and I simply *have* to find him before the police get hold of him."

"What's the matter?"

"He certainly got the agency in Dutch. They're talking about revoking our license."

"Why, isn't that too bad?"

"Too bad!" Bertha exclaimed, and then choked up with feeling.

"I'm sorry," Elsie Brand said.

Bertha said, "You only have butter on half the steak."

"I thought perhaps you preferred yours without."

"Oh, go ahead," Bertha said. "I'm too nervous to diet tonight."

I heard the scrape of chairs, the sound of knives and forks. Standing there in the closet, the pangs of hunger were as acute as the pain of a toothache. Listening, I could tell exactly what was going on. That would be Elsie cutting the steak now. She was putting a juicy, steaming piece on Bertha Cool's plate.

"Some asparagus tips?" she asked.

"Please," Bertha said.

"And you'll try some of this avocado salad?"

"Certainly. And plenty of potato chips."

"Pull off a piece of that French bread—but look out. It's hot."

I heard Elsie laugh, heard the scrape of a plate against another plate.

And then knuckles pounded on the door.

"Now what?" Bertha asked.

"I don't know," Elsie said, and then added with a flash of inspiration, "You don't suppose that's Donald, do you?"

"It may be."

Elsie Brand called through the door, "Who is it, please?"

"Never mind stalling around. Open up."

I knew that voice. It was Lieutenant Lisman.

Elsie Brand opened the door.

Bertha Cool said, "Well, pickle me for a peach!"

I heard Lisman laugh. "Rather a job trailing you here, Mrs. Cool, but we knew you were going to see Donald Lam. Where is he?"

"How the hell should I know?"

Lisman's laugh was impolite and skeptical.

Elsie Brand said, "Mrs. Cool came to ask me if I knew where he was."

"And stay to dinner," Lisman said.

"Yes. I invited her."

"How often has Mrs. Cool been to your apartment in the last two years?" Lisman asked.

"Well, I don't know as I could say—"

"Has she ever been here before?"

"Why—er—"

"Can you ever remember any time when she's been here before? Don't lie now."

Bertha Cool said, "What's that got to do with it? I'm here now."

"Exactly," Lisman said. "You're here now. Where did Donald Lam hide when he heard my knock at the door?"

Bertha laughed, and said, "What a great big gorilla you are. Just a dumb ape. You think he heard your knock on the door and ran to hide. Phooey! You reason like a Key-stone Comedy Cop."

Lisman said affably, "Well, don't let me interrupt, girls. I haven't had dinner myself. Suppose we just declare a truce until we finish."

"What do you mean, truce?" Elsie Brand asked.

"A complete truce," he said, "until we've finished with the dessert. There is dessert, isn't there, beautiful?"

"Chocolate pie," Elsie Brand said. "You've got your nerve!"

Lieutenant Lisman said, "You certainly can cook steak. That's about the nicest-looking steak I've seen in a month of Sundays. Cut me a piece right in there next to the bone if you will. Go right ahead, Mrs. Cool. Don't mind me."

I heard the scrape of the carving knife on the plate.

I opened the closet door and said, "Don't give that flatfoot *all* that meat. After all, *I'm* in on this party."

chapter 16

LIEUTENANT LISMAN pushed back his plate, looked at it wistfully for a moment, then with his fork mashed together the last few flakes of pie crust and conveyed the fork to his mouth. "The truce is now over," he announced.

Bertha Cool lit a cigarette, looked at him steadily, and said, "I don't give a damn what you do with Donald, but remember one thing. *I* didn't know he was here."

Lisman laughed. "It's a marvelous line," he said, "but you can't do anything with it. I talked with Captain Garver, told him I thought I could find Lam by shadowing you. I shadowed you. I found Lam. It worked out just as I said. Now I suppose you want me to go to the captain and tell him that it was just a coincidence, that I just happened to stumble onto the man I wanted."

Bertha Cool said with feeling, "Damn!"

Elsie Brand said, "She really didn't know he was here, Lieutenant. Honest."

Lisman fixed her with moody, morose eyes in which there was, nevertheless, an indication that he had future plans for Elsie sometime when he had the time, and was trying to remind himself not to forget it.

She saw that look and averted her own eyes.

"As far as *you're* concerned, you'd better sit back in a corner and keep your mouth shut. You're in a spot."

"I don't see why."

"*You* knew he was here."

She didn't say anything.

"And that he was a fugitive from justice."

"How was I to know he was a fugitive from justice? He told me he'd parked the agency car in front of a fire plug. Is it a crime to cook dinner for a man who's parked a car in front of a fire plug?"

"What was he doing here?"

She hesitated.

Bertha smacked her palm down on the table and said, "*I* know what he was doing here."

"Yes?" Lisman asked.

"He's fallen for her." Bertha sniffed. "Usually it's the other way around. They fall for him. This time, he went overboard. I make him a partner in the business, and the first thing he does is to raise her salary."

"How nice!" Lisman said.

"Isn't it?" Bertha Cool agreed sarcastically.

Elsie Brand got up from the table and said, "Now listen, you folks have barged in and eaten my dinner. I don't mind cooking, but I *hate* doing dishes. You're not going to walk out and leave me holding the dish cloth. Mrs. Cool, you've got to help me wipe dishes. Lieutenant, you can sit and smoke. Donald, you help clean off the table."

Bertha Cool said indignantly, "Well, I like that! You're working for me, young woman—or has that fact escaped you since you've surreptitiously been entertaining my partner?"

Elsie Brand said doggedly, "I'm working for you. That fact hasn't escaped me. You barged in for dinner. You're going to help with the dishes. Donald, pick up that platter and bring it along."

Elsie scooped up half a dozen dishes, scraped and stacked them. Her eyelid fluttered in an all but imperceptible signal.

I took the platter and carried it out to the kitchen.

Lieutenant Lisman came to stand in the door, looking the situation over. He said, "Got a key to that back door, sister?"

"Yes," Elsie Brand snapped. "You might even see it in the lock if you looked hard."

Lisman walked over, locked the back door, extracted the key, and put it in his pocket.

"I've got some food that's got to go out in the cooler on the back porch," Elsie protested.

"Well, get it all together," he said with a grin. "Then I'll open the door and you can put it out. But we wouldn't want Donald to get restless feet, would we?"

He walked back to the other room.

Elsie Brand said in a low voice, "The dumb-waiter over there behind the tub. I think you can make it if you take out that middle shelf. Do it when I'm in the other room."

She bustled back into the other room. I heard her scraping dishes once more.

I crawled in the dumb-waiter. It was an awkward position, but I went down, feeling that my toes and knees were about to be sliced off at any time, waiting for the roar that would mark Lieutenant Lisman's discovery that he'd been outsmarted.

I seemed to take an interminable time getting down to the bottom of the chute. I pressed against the door. A spring catch held it so it wouldn't open. I got my shoulder against it, and forced the spring catch back.

A door from a basement opened into an areaway with

iron stairs ascending to the street level. I walked up these stairs casually, fighting back a desire to run. Lisman would be hot on the scent any minute now.

Bertha Cool had parked the agency car in front of the apartment house. The car was locked, but I had a key which fitted both the ignition and the lock on the trunk. It wasn't the best place on earth, but I didn't have time to pick and choose.

I unlocked the trunk, raised the lid, and got inside. I had to double up, with my knees touching my chin, my head pushed down between my shoulders. I released the metal catches which held the trunk open. The lid fell down with a reassuring thud, and I was enclosed in stuffy darkness. The catch had snapped, and I was locked in.

I settled down to wait. A piece of metal was digging into my ankle, and one of the sliding arms which had held the trunk upright was pressing against my shoulder. It seemed that I was there five minutes before anything happened. During that time I wondered what would happen if Lisman took Bertha to headquarters and left the car there. I felt it wouldn't take more than an hour of that cramped confinement to kill me.

Then I heard voices. The man's voice was angry and threatening.

I heard Bertha Cool say sharply, "No such thing."

They were coming closer. They paused on the sidewalk almost even with the trunk. I could hear every word of the conversation.

Lieutenant Lisman said, "I tell you he was under arrest. You're going to find out that it's a serious thing to escape when you're under arrest. You're also going to find out it's damned serious to aid and abet anyone in escaping."

"Bosh," Bertha said.

"You helped him escape."

"You're making a lot of noise with your mouth," Bertha said. "I was sitting in the room with you all the time."

He thought that over. "I might have some difficulty convincing a jury that *you* helped him escape, but I know you did it."

Bertha Cool said, "Listen, sweetheart, I don't give a damn what you think. The only thing that concerns me is what twelve men in a jury box will think."

"Well, I can get that secretary of yours. I have her lashed to the mast. *She* helped him escape. That makes her an accessory."

"Escape from what?" Bertha asked.

"From me."

"And who the hell are you?"

"I happen to be the law."

"You didn't say so."

"What do you mean?"

"You didn't put him under arrest."

"What are you talking about?"

Bertha Cool said, "I'm talking about what happened. You came in there all filled with pride in your superb intelligence. You were oozing with triumph. You announced that you were going to stay for dinner, and there'd be a truce while we were eating. Donald came out of the closet. There was a truce on while you were eating. You never told him he was under arrest."

"He knew what I meant," Lisman said, his voice suddenly robbed of all its assurance.

"Bosh!" Bertha told him. "I never studied law, but Donald Lam did. There are certain things you have to do to place a man under arrest. You have to take him into custody, either figuratively or literally. You have to let him know that you're representing the law and that he's under arrest, charged with a certain crime."

"Well, I made a substantial compliance with all the requirements."

Bertha laughed and said, "You're a sucker!"

"What do you mean?"

"Making the case turn on that point. That means a couple of smart criminal lawyers will start taking you to pieces in front of a jury, commenting on the slipshod manner in which you discharge your official duties. The newspapers will pick it up. The officer who's so damn hungry he can't resist barging in on a dinner, declaring a truce until it's over, and then having his man skip out while he's sitting back from the table, rubbing his stomach, and picking his teeth!"

Lisman didn't say anything. When Bertha spoke again, I could tell from the triumphant barb in her voice that Lisman had given enough evidence of his consternation so she felt she could press home her advantage. "What's more, it looks like hell. The spectacle of a big officer like you mooching a dinner from a hard-working stenographer, then trying to arrest a pint-sized kid, and having the kid give him the slip. *You* going to charge me with being an accessory, and aiding and abetting a prisoner to escape. Nuts! You're going to keep your mouth shut about the whole business. And if I hear so much as a peep out of you, I'm damned if *I* don't tell the whole business to the news-papers. Now you think that over for a while."

I felt the springs of the car sway as Bertha jerked the door open and heaved herself indignantly in behind the wheel, sitting down hard on the cushions.

Lisman didn't say anything while she was inserting the key in the ignition lock and starting the engine.

Bertha had a habit of clashing gears when she started a car. Heaven knows how she did it. I'd deliberately tried chattering the gears in the agency car a dozen times, and had never been able to do it. No matter how I worked my clutch pedal and gear shift, the car would slip into low or second with perfect silence. But Bertha had some peculiar technique which made them clash almost every time.

Lieutenant Lisman was starting to say something just as the gears ground, then snapped home. The sudden lurch almost threw me against the trunk; then Bertha Cool was out in traffic, driving with that peculiar series of jerks which indicated she was alternating her foot between the brake pedal and the foot throttle.

I waited until her driving indicated she was getting away from the congested district with its succession of traffic signals, and then moved my hands around on the floor of the trunk until I found a jack handle. I picked it up and started a rhythmic series of thumps against the body of the car.

I felt the machine swerve as Bertha swung into the curb and slowed. I kept up the steady insistent pounding at the same regular intervals. The car stopped. I laid off.

I waited until Bertha was at the back of the car. I heard her say in an undertone, "Fry me for an oyster! I'd have sworn that was a flat tire!"

"It is," I said.

Bertha snapped back at me automatically without stopping to think, "You're a liar!" Then I heard her give a surprised gasp, and say, "Where the hell are you?"

I didn't say anything on the off chance some pedestrian might be passing, but left it to Bertha Cool to figure it out. It took her a matter of seconds; then she went back to climb in the car once more and start driving. This time she turned, apparently off the main highway, and finally, after two more turns, brought the car to a stop. She got out, came back, and opened the trunk.

"The nerve of you, you little rat," she said.

I eased myself out of my cramped position, slid to the curb, found that Bertha had turned down a dark side street. A block and a half away, the traffic was streaming briskly along the boulevard. Here, there were a few cars parked in front of residences and small apartments, but virtually no traffic.

Bertha said, "They're going to put *you* in a nice little room with bars all up and down the front of it, and you'll have a chance to slow down. Ever since you hit this agency, you've been skirting the edges of state prison and dragging me after you. The pace keeps getting faster and faster until I feel like—like a fly on the edge of a phonograph record."

When she saw I was grinning, she got madder than ever.

I said, "You're in too far now to back out. Get in the car and let's go."

"Where are we going?"

"To Corbin Harmley's apartment. If we get a lucky break, we'll find him at home. If we don't, we've got to use some pretext to get him there."

Bertha said, "You're too hot to be around. You're a legal leper. I don't want any part of you, Donald."

"It isn't what you want that counts. It's what you get."

"Well, I don't intend to get any part of you."

I said, "His address is the Albatross Apartments."

"I don't give a damn if it's the White House."

"We haven't got any time to lose."

"All right then, you take the car and go ahead. *I'll* get a taxi. I have an appointment with a fish tomorrow morning, and I don't like the inside of jails."

I said, "If I see him alone, it's his word against mine as to what was said. If you're there, it's two against one. You're in so deep now, backing up won't get you out."

Her eyes gittered. "You're always dragging me into it, aren't you?"

"After all, you have a half interest in the agency."

I walked around and got in behind the steering-wheel. "Get in," I told her.

Bertha slid in beside me, breathing heavily, like a person who's been climbing a flight of stairs. She didn't say anything all the way to the Albatross Apartments.

chapter 17

THE ALBATROSS was a swanky place with a doorman who looked like a field marshal, smart bellboys with the name

180

Albatross embroidered on the collars of their uniforms, and miniature albatrosses in white sewed on the left breast of their jackets. A haughty, supercilious clerk indicated plainly visitors were expected to announce themselves.

"Is Mr. Harmley in?"

"I'll see. What was the name?"

"Mrs. Cool and Donald Lam."

The clerk turned toward the switchboard. I kept my fingers crossed hard. Harmley was in. I heard the clerk say, "Good evening, Mr. Harmley. Mrs. Cool and a Donald Lam are waiting in the lobby."

I thought from the expression on the clerk's face Harmley was hesitating, then the clerk said, "Very well, Mr. Harmley."

He hung up the telephone. "You are to go up. It's apartment 621. Mr. Harmley said he was just leaving to keep an appointment, but he'll be able to give you a few minutes."

"That's fine," I said.

We walked over to the elevators. There were two. I said to Bertha, "Take this elevator to the sixth floor. I'll come up in the other."

"I don't get you."

"Never mind, hustle aboard."

Bertha gave me a glowering look and got aboard the elevator. The colored elevator boy looked at me curiously, then shot the cage up. The other elevator was on its road down. I watched the indicator, saw it pause briefly at the sixth floor, then the needle swung down to the fourth, stopped, went to the second, stopped, and came down to the lobby. Corbin Harmley pushed his way out of the elevator and started walking rapidly toward the door. He had his hat on and an overcoat over his arm.

"Harmley."

He whirled at the sound of my voice. "Oh, yes, there you are. Wasn't there someone with you?"

181

"Mrs. Cool."

"Oh, yes."

I said, "She went up to the sixth floor. I waited down here—so in case you'd misunderstood the clerk, we wouldn't miss you."

He said quickly, "Why, I understood the clerk to say you'd be waiting here in the lobby. I have a very important appointment. I can only give you just a second or two. I—" He broke off and looked at his watch significantly.

I said, "We'll go back up to the sixth floor. Bertha's waiting up there."

"I'm afraid I haven't time."

"It might be better for us to talk up there than down here."

He glanced toward the clerk's desk and said, "Oh, well, I'll take a chance on being a minute or two late. Come on."

We rode back up in the elevator. Bertha, standing indignantly waiting, sized up the situation as I got out with Harmley. Some of the anger left her eyes.

"We talk in your apartment or here?" I asked.

His hesitation was hardly perceptible. "Why, in my apartment, of course. I only have a few minutes, however. Perhaps later on I can give you more detailed information—"

"Come on," I interrupted. "It won't take long."

He led the way down to his apartment, unlocked the door, and stood aside for Bertha to enter. She walked in. He waited for me to follow, but I used a gentle pressure on his arm to get him in next. I brought up the rear.

"Well?" he asked, standing there looking from one to the other, and not asking us to sit down.

I said, "I have something to tell you. I'm not really a friend of the Devarest family. Up to a short time ago, I'd never seen Nadine Croy."

"How interesting."

"I am, in fact, a private detective."

He broke out laughing then. "Is this supposed to surprise me?"

"Why not?"

"Good heavens, give me credit for *some* intelligence. The whole situation fairly screamed that you were detectives: the way you took charge of things, the ideas you had about that garage door. Come, come, Lam. Don't tell me that friend-of-the-family business was assumed for *my* benefit. I thought that perhaps you didn't want the servants gossiping, but the idea that you thought you were fooling me is absolutely preposterous—particularly when one only needs to consult the telephone directory to find the name of 'B. Cool—Confidential Investigations' and learn that Donald Lam is her right-hand man."

"Partner," I said.

"So you've been promoted, eh? My congratulations—to both of you."

He was very suave, very much master of himself and of the situation now.

I said, "In my capacity as private detective, I made rather a complete investigation."

"Certainly. That's what you were being paid to do."

"In the course of that investigation, I went up to the probate clerk's office and looked up several large estates. I did a little telephoning to try and find out if any person who answered your description had perhaps borrowed money from the decedent a few months before his death, and then gone to South America, only to return the day after the man died. Do you want names, dates, telephone numbers and amounts, or is that a sufficient statement to break the ice?"

The assurance which had given him such patronizing impregnability was leaking out fast.

"Well?" I asked.

He said, "Let's all sit down."

Bertha walked over to the center of the room, picked the easiest chair, and dropped into it. I kept the position which was between Harmley and the door.

"What do you want?" Harmley asked.

"You might give us the complete facts. We can get them in a very short time by communicating with the police. It might save trouble all around if you gave them to us now."

He pushed his hands down in his pockets, stood looking moodily at Bertha Cool. Then he turned to me. He said, "You left yourself wide open. I looked you up, and found out all about you. It never occurred to me that you'd do the same by me."

"That was most unfortunate—for you."

"So it seems."

"However, there's no use stalling about it."

He said, "Perhaps we could talk a little business."

"Perhaps we could."

Harmley asked, "How could we work this out?"

"I don't know."

He said, "My motto is live and let live."

"It's a good motto."

"I could make this all right for you."

"Could you?"

"Yes."

"I'd have to know all the details before I'd know what to say."

He thought that over for a while, then said, "Well, after all, why not?"

"Why not?" I asked.

He seemed to be trying to convince himself. He said, in that expressionless voice a man uses when he hasn't any particular audience to address, "If you've got that much dope on me, you can get the whole business. I couldn't hurt anything by telling you the whole story."

I warned Bertha with a glance to keep quiet. The man was selling himself out. There was no need of interpolating any comments.

"After all," he went on in that same monologue, "Walter Croy would double-cross me in a minute—and I'd warned him about this."

I sat perfectly still, not saying anything, not moving, hardly breathing.

Harmley's eyes weren't even on me. They were studying the pattern on the carpet. "I suppose I should have covered up more. I got too careless."

He pushed his hands down in his pockets. There was an interval of silence which lasted for thirty seconds.

Harmley said, "I'd like to have you see this from my viewpoint. I don't suppose you will. After all, what I'm doing isn't so bad."

I knew if I could get him talking about himself and justifying himself, I'd get more details than if I tried to bore right in. I glanced at Bertha, then said, "How did you happen to get started with this, Harmley?"

"That's the thing," he said, almost eager in his attempt to justify himself to himself and to us. "It sort of grew. I was a younger brother. I had an older brother who had the knack of selling anybody anything." A look of bitterness came over his face. His mouth, for the moment, grew surly.

"I suppose your brother got all the breaks," I said.

"I'll say he did. He kidded the schoolteachers along. He kidded Mother. He didn't do quite so well with Dad, but Dad couldn't hold out against all the feminine pressure. Well, anyway, I was left to shift for myself. The brother got all the education, all the opportunities—and then started playing the races and gambling, forged checks which the old man had to make good. The guy finally busted the family—and they still think he's a little tin god, that he just didn't get the breaks, and—oh, what's the use?"

"There isn't any," I told him.

"Well, I saw what could be done by working on credulous women—but I didn't see it right away. When I left home and went out in the world, I was pretty sour. I wasn't getting anywhere. Then I got acquainted with a woman. She began to feel sorry for me. She was married. Her husband was older than she was. She fell for me pretty hard, started giving me money, lectured me about being surly and sullen and said I should cultivate my personality. She started paying for my education. God, I even took voice lessons. I was crazy about her. She'd never had any children. Guess I was sort of her son, her lover, and something she was training all at once."

"What happened to her?" Bertha asked.

He looked up to meet Bertha's eyes. His face became hard and bitter. "Her husband found out about it, and killed her," he said slowly.

Bertha's face showed the way she felt. "What did you do to the husband?"

"Not a damn thing," he said, and, watching his hands, I could see the fists clench until the skin grew tight and white across his knuckles.

"Why not?" I asked.

"There was nothing I could do. Understand, he wasn't so crude as to take a gun and bump her off. He murdered her in a diabolically clever way. It could have been either him or me that did the job. If I'd stirred anything up, he'd have pinned it on me."

"I don't see how that could have happened," Bertha said.

He said bitterly, "She died while she was with me—in my arms."

"Poison?" I asked.

"Yes. He'd found out she was leaving for a rendezvous with me, but pretended not to know anything about it. He said he was leaving for a lodge meeting. It was her birthday. He opened a bottle of champagne. They had a couple of toasts together, then he left, and she came to me.

It was almost half an hour before the thing hit her. At first, we didn't know what it was. Then she realized. I wanted to get a doctor, but she insisted she was going to go home and telephone a doctor from there. She didn't make it."

Once more there was an interval of silence. I waited until I saw some of the bitterness leave his face and a wistful expression soften the lines. "What happened after that?" I asked.

He said, "I was half crazy for a while. She'd left me with some money. It should have lasted me for quite a little while. It didn't. I tried to forget about things with booze. That didn't work. It never does. Well, I had to eat. I got a job in a café. They said I was to be an entertainer. It turned out they wanted me for a gigolo.

"I didn't care too much about the job, but it was all right at that. I began to practice some of the lessons Olive had taught me, trying to impress people, to keep laughing and smiling, and hold the thought that the world was my oyster. I put my stuff across. There was good money in it.

"I began to learn something about a certain type of woman, the woman who has a successful husband, so fascinated making money he pays no attention to his wife. They're the loneliest women on earth. Marriage ties them up to a certain extent. They're dependent on a man who cares nothing for them. They want something to do. Above all, they want to be noticed. They want to feel that they're not just an animated clothes rack."

"And so they go to places and hire gigolos?" I asked.

"Yes, and if the gigolo plays it right, he gets easy pickings."

"I take it you played it right?"

"Of course I did—and don't think I didn't give them value received either. I made them happy. Well, then I drifted into this racket. I stumbled onto it almost by accident."

"How did you get your prospects?" I asked.

"I'd watch the obituary columns. When some prominent man would die, I could tell from reading the obituary whether there was a chance to put my stuff across."

"Then you'd be a man whom the husband had befriended?"

"That's right. Shortly after the death I'd write a letter of condolence and ask permission to call and express my sympathies in person. A woman can't very well shut out a chap who wants to tell her how marvelous her husband was, and repay a loan."

I nodded.

"After that," he said, "it's easy sailing. You're dealing with a woman who has suffered the emotional shock of suddenly finding herself a widow, a woman who has been more or less neglected, a woman who is slightly bitter about marriage, a woman who sees the sands of life slipping through her fingers, a woman who has seen her mind narrow as her hips broaden."

Bertha Cool flushed angrily, started to say something, then caught my eye and kept quiet.

"How long had you been associated with Croy?"

"Quite a while. Walter was in another branch of the same racket. He worked his stuff on the widow of a man Dr. Devarest had been treating. Devarest got the whole dope, including a sworn statement by the woman. That held Walter for a while; then the woman died. Her statement was the only evidence Dr. Devarest had. Walter thought if he could get that, he'd be okay."

"Then what happened?"

"Then Dr. Devarest's safe was robbed."

"Walter Croy had something to do with that?"

"No."

"How do you know?"

"I know absolutely."

"That doesn't mean anything to me."

"When you know what happened after that, you'll understand that he didn't."

"What happened after that?"

"After Dr. Devarest died, Walter didn't know where that statement was. He thought at first Mrs. Devarest had it. He didn't think she'd ever connect me with him. Nadine had seen me one night. I'd called on Walter. That had been years ago. We didn't think there was any chance she'd remember about that. Walter insisted I pull the old gag with the widow, to see if she was the one who had the dope out of the safe."

"What made him think she had it?"

"He couldn't imagine who else could have taken it."

"Did Walter think Mrs. Devarest would rob the safe of her own stuff?"

"Walter didn't take me entirely into his confidence. He's closemouthed on some things. But he knew pretty much what was going on. Devarest had started to play around with his wife's secretary. Walter thought Mrs. Devarest had taken a tumble to that and had decided to frame her with the theft of the jewels."

"You can tell me some more about that."

"Mrs. Devarest got the jewels out of the safe. She planted evidence so Nollie Starr would be blamed. Dr. Devarest realized that. As soon as he found out about the theft, he arranged with the Starr girl to beat it and keep under cover until he had time to straighten things out."

"Then how about the jewels?"

"The wife had the jewels. Devarest knew it. He let the Starr girl skip out while he was trying to find how thoroughly his wife had framed her. While he was doing that, he quietly snooped around and found out where his wife had the jewels hidden. He got them out of the hiding-place and arranged to have them returned under such circumstances that it would break the frame-up on the Starr girl. He never lived to do it."

189

"Why?"

He looked me straight in the eye and said, "*You* should know."

"What do you mean by that?"

"He was murdered before he had a chance to do anything."

"What makes you think he was murdered?"

"The same thing that makes you think he was."

"Who killed him?"

He made a little gesture of dismissal with his shoulders.

"And what did you do?"

"I convinced myself the wife either didn't have what Walter was afraid of, or, if she did, she had destroyed it. I reported to Walter and he started proceedings."

"That was all you were supposed to do?"

"That was all I was supposed to do for *Walter*."

"But you stayed on to work for yourself?"

"That's right. Colette fell for that story about the loan, fell for it so hard that I saw no reason why I shouldn't cash in on it. I thought perhaps Nadine had recognized me at first, but after a while, when she didn't say anything, I felt I was getting by. I tried a few leads to see if she'd talked with you. You were too smart for me. You questioned me about what might have been in the safe, and I gave you a lead which would make you think the dope Devarest had on Walter was a photograph. You pretended to fall for that so thoroughly, you had me fooled. I decided you were dumb. I decided to stay on, and make a cleanup under your nose. Well, I underestimated you. You're slick —but we can do business. I'm not going to be greedy, and, as far as I'm concerned, Walter's out of it. You let me go ahead. You won't have to show your hand in it at all. All you have to do is keep your mouth shut, and you get a fifty-fifty split."

"How do I know I get the split?" I asked.

"You could turn me in if you didn't get it."

"And have you make a blackmail squawk?"

He said, "You'd know when I got it. You could be on hand to get yours. I'd play fair with you. I'd have to."

I pretended to think it over for a while.

He said, eagerly, "She wants me to look after some of her investments. I tell you, Lam, I've got this thing all sewed up. It's just the same as money in the bank. I'll handle it in such a way it'll be entirely legal. Get her to invest in certain stocks. No one will ever be able to prove that I controlled those stocks or got a cut out of the investment. No one will ever be able to prove that you got anything out of it. You can make more money in a few weeks trailing along with me than you can by running a detective agency for a year."

"And leave Mrs. Devarest strapped?" I asked.

"I don't leave them strapped. I'm too smart for that. If I did, they'd go to their lawyers and make a squawk. I only take a few thousand. I'll take perhaps fifteen or twenty from Mrs. Devarest. You'd get a cut of ten thousand."

Bertha squirmed nervously.

I said, "I'll have to talk it over with my partner."

"When will you let me know?"

"Sometime tomorrow."

He said, "Remember it's absolutely on the up-and-up. Dr. Devarest left his wife something like two hundred thousand dollars—by the time you figure the estate and the life insurance. She'll never miss twenty or thirty."

"You've boosted the ante."

"Well," he said, "she can stand a touch of thirty, and if I've got to split fifty-fifty with you, I'd have to make it thirty to make it worth *my* while."

"And Walter?"

"To hell with him. He gets no split at all. After all, he was interested in this other matter. He's found out he's in the clear on that now, and he'll get his out of Nadine."

I got up and nodded to Bertha. "Okay, Bertha, that's the proposition. Let's talk it over."

Harmley solicitously bowed us to the door. "You think it over," he said anxiously. "You'll never have a chance to pick up fifteen grand any easier—and it's perfectly legitimate."

I took Bertha Cool's arm. "We'll think it over," I told him.

"I don't see what you've got to think over."

"You wouldn't. Come on, Bertha."

Out in the corridor, Bertha Cool said to me, "Lieutenant Lisman is going to be combing the city for you. You've either got to crack this thing, or else get away from me. You'll have me in a hospital by morning."

I said, "You're giving me an idea."

"What?"

"The one place Lisman would never look for me."

"Where?"

"In a hospital."

"And how are you going to get into a hospital?"

I said, "That's a detail. It may cost money."

Bertha's face twisted into a wry contortion. "You think money grows on trees."

I said, "Of course, I can stay with you, if you'd prefer."

She said hastily, "How much will it cost?"

"Oh, perhaps a hundred, or a hundred and fifty."

Bertha sighed.

"In cash," I said.

Bertha stood in a hallway in front of the elevators, opened her purse, counted out a hundred and fifty dollars in currency, and slammed it in my palm.

chapter 18

DR. GELDERFIELD came to the door himself in response to my ring. His expression showed the annoyance of a professional man at being disturbed when he is off duty; but when he saw who it was, his face lit up.

"Well, well, it's Donald Lam, the mighty little fighter. Come in, come in. This is the maid's night off, and I have to answer the doorbell myself. I always dread this night, because so many people disturb a doctor for trivial reasons. Come right in and sit down."

I followed him into a reception hallway in which were several chairs. He said, "I fixed this up so emergency patients can have a place to wait. I have a small room in back where I can perform minor surgery. We'll go back to the living-quarters where we can stretch out and relax. I hope you aren't in too much of a hurry."

"I'm not in too much of a hurry as long as I'm here."

"That's splendid. I want a long talk with you. I have something on my mind that's worrying me—my patient and your client—Mrs. Devarest, you know."

"What about Mrs. Devarest?" I asked.

Dr. Gelderfield frowned. "I'm worried about her. Come in here and sit down. How about a drink? I won't join you myself because I never can tell when I'll be called out on an emergency."

"I could use a Scotch and soda."

"Sit right there. I'll fix it. I have everything here except the ice. I'll get that from the icebox. Sit right down and make yourself at home. I'm sorry I was rather brusque with you the time I called you out to my car. I didn't realize then—well, just what sort of person you were. Just wait there and I'll get the liquor."

I stretched out in a chair. The room was restful, with deep, soft chairs, a subdued lighting, walls lined with bookcases, a big table well covered with magazines and books, individual shaded floor lamps standing back of the chairs, humidors ready to hand, cigarettes and matches in profusion—the sort of room to live in.

The room was sweet with the odor of fragrant tobacco, had the same atmosphere of having been well used that clings to a good pair of worn boots. One could relax here, the rush, the noise, and the bustle of the outside world being shut off by modern, soundproof walls. An air-conditioning unit kept the room at a comfortable temperature and humidity.

Out in the kitchen, I could hear Dr. Gelderfield dropping ice cubes into a bowl.

He came back with a tray, a bottle of old Scotch, a bottle of club soda, a big glass full of ice cubes, and a straw holder for the glass so that moisture wouldn't get on my fingers.

"Help yourself, Lam," he said, placing the tray on a little coffee table by my chair. "I'm sorry I can't join you. Mix it to suit yourself. At least, I can enjoy watching you. I can't get over that splendid exhibition you put up. It was a grand fight. Bad for my patient. I should have rushed her right back into the house, but I'll admit I was momentarily neglectful of my duty. You have marvelous speed and co-ordination. Where did you learn to fight?"

I laughed and said, "I learned it the hard way. Everyone used to beat up on me. Bertha Cool put up money for jujitsu lessons. They did some good. In one of my cases I spent quite a bit of time with a slap-happy prize fighter who was imbued with the idea of putting me in training. Some of it stuck."

"I'll tell the world it did! Always like to see a little man give it to a big fellow—guess it's the way we all sympathize with the underdog. It was a neat exhibition. Can't get over thinking of it."

I poured myself a drink.

"You were going to say something about Mrs. Devarest?"

He nodded, started to say something, then checked himself, and regarded me thoughtfully. At length, he said, "There are certain ethics of the profession. I couldn't discuss a patient's symptoms or my diagnosis with you—unless I had the consent of that patient."

I didn't say anything.

He waited a moment to emphasize the importance of what he was going to say and then went on. "But I happen to know that you were employed by my patient to make a certain investigation. My patient has instructed me to co-operate with you to the fullest extent. Therefore, *if* carrying to a successful conclusion the work which you were doing necessitates knowing something about the condition of my patient, I would feel free to answer such specific questions as you might ask touching on that particular point. You see what I'm getting at. Her authorization to assist you in any way would permit me to disclose facts about her condition that might have a direct bearing on the work you're doing."

He waited then for me to ask a question. I could see that he was hoping I'd ask the right one.

"Is Mrs. Devarest necessarily confined to her bed and wheel chair?"

"Only for the purpose of reducing the strain on her nerves and heart, and keeping her mind occupied with herself—which, for certain reasons, seems to be important just now."

He placed a subtle emphasis on the "certain reasons."

I said, "She apparently felt, and with some reason, that her secretary, Nollie Starr, was in a peculiar relationship with her husband. Would that have caused any unusually bitter enmity against Miss Starr—bearing in mind the fact that the woman's nervous condition and the shock that she has received have made her perhaps a bit unstable?"

His eyes sparkled. "You are asking the question that I was hoping you would ask. That opens the door for me to tell you something that I think is very important. Her hatred of Miss Starr is becoming a very definite, tangible menace to her health. She is beginning to brood over it. I am doing everything in my power trying to get her mind more on herself and less on the Starr woman."

I said, "Well, honest confession is good for the soul. After all, you're in a peculiar position here, and I may as well report to you before I report to my client."

"What has happened? Something out of the ordinary?"

"Yes. I went to Nollie Starr's apartment. I let myself in with a passkey because I wanted to look around."

"What for?"

I said, "I'll go a step behind that. I put a little pressure to bear on Bayley, the chauffeur. I found out that he'd had a criminal record."

"So I understand," Dr. Gelderfield said. "The police have released a statement Bayley made. To me it sounded preposterous. I'm surprised to hear there's anything to it."

"I put it up to him to get those gems for me."

"What made you think he could get them for you?"

"I had reason to believe he could."

"Did he?"

"Yes."

"Where are they?"

"I have them."

"You haven't told Mrs. Devarest?"

"No."

"Did Miss Starr—" He paused.

"Go ahead."

"—have anything to do with the disappearance of those gems?"

"I think she did."

"I was afraid so," he said. "You haven't as yet said anything to Mrs. Devarest about the stones?"

"No."

"Or given her any inkling as to where you got them, how you got them, or in what way Miss Starr might have been concerned in their disappearance?"

"No."

"Don't do it. We'll have to work up some other way of handling the matter. It would have a devastating effect on my patient's mind."

"Perhaps she knows already."

"I don't think so. I think I'd have learned of it if she knew."

"But there's a possibility that you might not?"

"Yes, a possibility." He thought for a moment, then added, "A distinct possibility."

"All right," I said. "Now, I'm coming to my confession."

"What is it?"

"I went to Miss Starr's apartment. I let myself in with a passkey. At first, I thought the apartment was deserted. It should have been at the hour in the morning when I entered. It wasn't. Someone was there."

"Who?"

"Nollie Starr."

"What did she do?"

"Nothing. She was dead."

"Dead!"

"Yes."

"How long had she been dead?"

"Not very long. She'd been strangled. A pink-colored corset string had been doubled and knotted around her throat. The handle of a potato masher had been inserted in the string and twisted. I don't know what the post-mortem will show, but I wouldn't be surprised if she'd been clubbed, perhaps into unconsciousness, possibly by a blow struck from behind with the potato masher."

For a moment his face showed surprised incredulity, then his lips twitched. He evidently wanted to say something, but fought against the impulse.

I said, "The murder had been committed only a few minutes before I arrived. The body was still quite warm. There was no pulse. I loosened the cord and telephoned for a Pulmotor. Then I walked out. There was nothing more I could do. A scrubwoman in the hallway saw me go out. That and a couple of other things have put the police on my trail."

"But, good heavens, man, can't you establish your innocence? Surely murderers don't ring up and ask aid for their victims."

"They might," I said, "if they were certain the victims were dead. It would be a good dodge. At least, that's the way the police will look at it. And regardless of what may happen eventually, right now I can't afford to be put out of circulation."

"Why not?"

"Because I think I'm getting ready to close the whole case. There'll be developments within the next twenty-four hours that will tell me whether I'm right. I can't afford to spend those twenty-four hours in a cell. That's where you come in."

"What do you want me to do?"

I said, "I'm calling on you. I've had a terrific nervous shock. My heart is bad. My blood pressure is way up. I'm nervous and jittery. You're going to give me a sedative and send me to a hospital where I won't be disturbed. At the end of twenty-four hours, you hope I'll have recovered enough so the police can question me without jeopardizing my health. If I cheat on you and don't take the sedative, you won't know anything about it—not officially."

He was shaking his head even before I'd finished speaking. "I can't do that, not ethically."

"Why not? You haven't even examined me yet."

"You don't show any signs of having the symptoms you complain of. If I said I'd given you a sedative, I'd have to give you a sedative, a good hypodermic. If I did that, you'd sleep the clock around. You wouldn't be good for anything. You'd probably wake up with a heavy, drugged feeling. I can't do it."

I said, "Let's think this thing over a little more carefully."

"It doesn't make any difference what you say, Lam. I

simply can't do it. I'd do anything I could conscientiously, but I can't do that."

"The weapon used was a potato masher," I said. "The thing that followed that up was a corset string. Hardly the weapons a man would use."

He saw what I was getting at now, and started arguing with me. "Why not?" he asked. "A man could have been smart enough to have used weapons that would have directed suspicion toward a woman."

"He could have, but the chances are ten to one he didn't."

"Well, even so—" He abruptly decided not to pursue that conversational vein.

I said, "The night Dr. Devarest was killed, you'll remember I went into Mrs. Devarest's bedroom. There was a corset on the back of a chair, one of those girdle affairs. It had pink strings in it."

"I can assure you, young man, that those are by no means unusual. Many women approaching middle age use figure supports of various kinds."

I held his eye. "Lieutenant Lisman is working on the case. It won't be long before he starts checking up on Mrs. Devarest. Let's suppose, just for the sake of the argument, he finds that the girdle she has been wearing is missing, or finds that the string has been removed from it. Let's further suppose he finds there's no potato masher in her kitchen."

"Preposterous!"

I lit a cigarette and sat smoking, saying nothing. The strain of the silence began to tell on him.

"Even so, it could have been a frame-up."

"It could have been. She's your patient. You're sticking up for her."

"I wouldn't stick up for a murderess just because she was my patient. But I know Mrs. Devarest—well. I know that it would be absolutely impossible for her to have done any such thing as you describe."

"Speaking only as a physician speaks of a patient?" I asked.

"Just what do you mean by that?"

"I had thought perhaps your feeling for her was a little less impersonal."

I resumed my cigarette, and let him do a little thinking. There was quite a pause.

"What," he asked, "can we do?"

I said, "That's better. *I* can't go to Mrs. Devarest's house, not now. In the first place, the police will be watching it. In the second place, even if they didn't pick me up, they'd find out I'd been there. If *I* should go and search the kitchen for a potato masher or make some excuse to look in the woman's bedroom to see if there was a string in her girdle, it would undo the very thing I'm trying to accomplish. But *you* could go very nicely. It wouldn't excite any comment. In fact, it would be entirely natural for the woman's physician to call on her. You could find, perhaps, that she needed a hypodermic. You'd have to go to the kitchen to boil some water. While you were there, you could quietly look around and see if you could locate a potato masher."

"Even if I couldn't, it wouldn't prove anything."

"Who does your cooking here?"

"Why, I eat most of my meals out. I have a housekeeper who keeps the place in order and cooks for my father. He's bedridden."

"Does she ever serve mashed potatoes?"

"Why?"

"There's probably a potato masher in your kitchen. You could slip it in your instrument bag; then if you couldn't find a potato masher in Mrs. Devarest's house, you could see to it that the police *did* find one."

He said in a shocked voice, "Lam, are you crazy? I'm a reputable physician and surgeon. I couldn't do anything like that."

I said, "Mrs. Devarest is your patient. She's your friend. She's my client. I'd like to make her forty thousand dollars and collect a percentage on it. We both have a keen personal interest in what's going to happen. You don't want her arrested right at this time and neither do I. I could stay here while you made the trip. When you got back, you could tell me what you'd found. Then you could send me to the hospital. While I was there, I could do some thinking."

"I couldn't do any of that ethically."

"There comes a time in the life of every physician when he has to remember that he's a man as well as a physician. Professional ethics are all right as a rule of guidance, but there are times when it's a lot more logical to toss ethics out of the window."

He got up and began to pace the floor. I kept on smoking my cigarette. He walked back and forth with nervous rapidity, occasionally cracking his knuckles. That made me fidgety and I got up and walked to the window. It was too dark to see anything.

Gelderfield must have changed his mind about a drink because I heard him open the Scotch and pour some out. I turned around in time to see him down a short one before he went out into the kitchen. I could hear him opening and closing drawers. I heard his steps on the stairs going to the second floor, heard him moving around in an upper bedroom; then he came back down the stairs into the kitchen again. Then, after a few seconds, he came back and picked up his black bag of surgical instruments.

"Find it?" I asked.

"I don't know whether I care to say anything—certainly not to commit myself. You've given me something to think about. You think the police will make a search of her kitchen?"

"Exactly."

"Good Lord, if the stores were only open, we could buy a dozen of the damn things at fifteen cents apiece."

"The police," I said, "will also take that into consideration."

He took his surgical bag out into the kitchen, came back with his mouth thin and straight. "All right, Lam, I'm going through with it. You've done something no one hitherto has been able to do—get me to violate the code of my profession."

"All right," I said, "get started. Do you want me to answer the phone?"

"You might take any calls that come in."

"It *might* not be so good," I told him.

"Suppose I want to call you?"

"In that event, ring up from a dial telephone. As soon as you hear the phone ring, hang up and break the connection. Wait sixty seconds, then call again. That will be my signal, the phone ringing once or perhaps twice, and then quitting. Then after sixty seconds, another call. I'll answer that second call."

He thought that over, then said, "Yes, I guess that's okay."

"And you'll send me to the hospital?"

"I'd have to give you a hypodermic."

"When a person is nervous and unsettled, don't you sometimes give them a hypodermic of sterile water and tell them it's morphine sulphate?"

His face lit up. "By George, yes!"

I said, "You could diagnose my case as nervous hysteria. I could be begging you for dope. You wouldn't want to give it to me. You could give me a hypo of sterile water. Under the influence of that, my nerves would begin to quiet. I'd show symptoms of drowsiness. You could—"

"Under those circumstances," he said, "I could call a nurse for you and put you to bed in my own house. You would, of course, be in the charge of the nurse, but once the nurse thought you were safely asleep, she wouldn't actually stay in the same room with you."

"Would there be some way of getting out of that room?"

"You could climb to the window, drop to the roof of the kitchen porch, let yourself down to the wooden rail, and—well, you'd be back within an hour, wouldn't you?"

"I'm not certain."

"Well, that's the best I can do for you, Lam."

"The nurse wouldn't be in on it?"

"Of course not. She'd think you were a bona fide patient who had settled into peaceful slumber following a hypodermic of what you thought was morphine sulphate."

"How long will it take you to get the nurse?"

"I can get one in twenty minutes."

"A good one?"

"Yes."

I motioned toward the door. "Get going. It takes you quite a while to get an idea, but when you once get it, it germinates nicely."

He picked up his bag, and walked rapidly out the door. A few moments later, I heard his automobile gliding along the driveway and picking up speed as it turned into the street.

I settled myself back in the depths of the big overstuffed chair, poured myself another drink of Scotch, added soda, and took a long drink. I lit a cigarette, took another good-sized drag of the whisky, and elevated my feet to the footstool. It seemed unusually quiet in the house. There was not so much as the creaking of a board, no sound of traffic from the outside world. The room was a veritable refuge from the noise and bustle that reigned beyond the air-conditioned silence of those protecting walls.

I finished my cigarette and my drink. I wondered if Dr. Gelderfield would lose his nerve—telephone a report of what was taking place—would he talk with Mrs. Devarest?

I stretched and yawned. A delicious warmth enveloped

me. I could realize how much a place like this meant to a doctor, a chance to relax where he could forget the responsibilities of his practice.

I looked at my wrist watch. My eyes had a little trouble bringing the hands into focus.

Something significant began to hammer at the back of my mind for attention. I didn't want to think about it. I tried to dismiss it from my mind and couldn't. Then suddenly the idea struck me with an impact which brought me up out of my chair.

I stumbled over the footstool, caught my balance, and walked rapidly back to the kitchen. There was a hallway back of the kitchen, a flight of back stairs going up to the second floor. I climbed those stairs. It was an effort. I entered an upper hallway and tried the first door on the right. It was evidently Dr. Gelderfield's bedroom. I went through a bathroom into an adjoining bedroom which was evidently a guest room. I stumbled against the side of the door as I went through into the corridor, crossed the corridor to the other side, and pushed a door open.

An emaciated man who must have been well in the seventies lay motionless on the bed with his eyes closed. There was a waxy sheen to his skin. His mouth was open. I stood over the bed, listening to him breathe.

He'd go without breathing for almost a minute, then start breathing heavily, gasping in air in deep breaths, then pause again for so long that I thought he'd quit for good.

I reached out my hand to touch his bony shoulder. I lost my balance and fell against him on the bed.

The man made no move, but kept up his peculiarly irregular breathing. I shook him. He moved uneasily. I shook him again. He flung up an arm. The hand struck my shoulder. I slapped him gently on the side of the jaw. He opened his eyes.

I said, "You're Dr. Gelderfield's father." My voice

sounded faint and far away.

It took him a minute to gather his faculties. He kept his eyes fastened on mine. I saw the lids start to flutter closed.

I shouted at him, "You're Dr. Gelderfield's father."

He opened his eyes wide and said, "Yes," in a flat, lifeless voice.

By concentrating with every bit of energy and will power at my command, I could hold my mind in focus. I said, "Dr. Devarest was treating you, wasn't he?"

"Yes."

"He isn't any more?"

"No. My son thought it would be better to wait for a while. Who—who are you?"

I said, "Dr. Devarest is dead."

Apparently the words meant nothing to him.

"Did you know he was dead?"

His eyes started to flutter shut. He said, "He hasn't been here for a week."

I shook him again. "When did you see him last? Was it Wednesday—after he'd been fishing?"

The man looked at me with eyes that seemed out of focus. "When he got back from fishing?" I asked.

I shook him. The man roused and said, "Yes. He'd been fishing. He and my son had a quarrel."

"What about?"

"Because his medicine wasn't doing me any good."

"Your son told you about that afterward?"

"Yes, but I heard the quarrel."

"Your son—told you what they were quarreling about?"

He started to answer me, then closed his eyes. The telephone downstairs rang twice, two quick rings. Then the ringing ceased.

That would be the first part of the signal. Dr. Gelderfield was on the line. I looked at the second hand of my wrist watch and couldn't bring my eyes to focus on it. I got up and started for the stairs. I collided with the side of the door. I tried to make speed down the stairs without falling, but my legs became tangled halfway down. I took a pounding, falling down the stairs. That helped jar my faculties into wakefulness. I started for the telephone. It began to ring again just as I reached it. That would be the second signal. Dr. Gelderfield was calling.

I picked up the receiver and, for a moment, couldn't think of the word a person was supposed to use when he started talking in the telephone. After a while, I said, "Yes."

Dr. Gelderfield's voice, crisply professional, came over the wire. "That you, Lam?"

"Yes."

"All right, Lam, I'm over here. The string that you thought might be missing is gone. You understand what I mean?"

"Yes."

"Well, don't worry about it. I took the whole girdle. The masher is in place. Do you understand?"

"Yes."

A note of sharp concern came into his voice. "Are you all right, Lam?"

"I—I guess so."

"You didn't take too much Scotch?"

"No—I don't know—no."

"You sound terribly tired."

"I am."

He said, "Lam, don't fail me now. There's too much at stake. You understand the risk I'm taking."

"Yes."

"Lam, have you been drinking?"

"Just one more—only one."

"You're certain that's all you've had?"

"Yes."

"A good-sized drink?"

"I—I guess so."

He said irritably, "Lam, you've had too much. You can't afford to let me down. Take that bottle of Scotch and pour it down the sink. Don't touch another drop. Promise me you'll do that, Lam."

I said thickly, "All right," and pushed the receiver hook down, cutting off the connection.

I tried to wait long enough for the connection to be terminated and the line cleared. There was a great roaring inside of my ears. My head seemed a huge globe which was turning slowly on an axis, gathering momentum as it spun around. I tried to stop it and couldn't. I reached out with my right hand to find something to hang onto and caught the thick cloth of one of the heavy drapes. I twisted my fist up in it, and hung on. Then I lifted my left hand. I knew that I had to dial Operator. I groped with my finger trying to find the last hole in the dial and slowly twisted it around. Then I let it go.

It seemed an hour from the time I released the dial until a feminine voice said crisply, "Operator."

"Police headquarters—hurry—murder."

I couldn't hear well. It seemed that a stream of water was pouring through my ears, falling on my eardrums like some great cataract. Coming through this roaring sound, I heard a man's voice say, "Police headquarters."

I said, "Lieutenant Lisman—Lisman—murder."

The receiver seemed to echo the words, "Lisman—Lisman—this is Lisman. . . . Hello. This is Lisman. What do you want?"

I gathered all my faculties into determined focus and said, "This is Donald Lam. . . . I'm at Dr. Gelderfield's house. I've poisoned Mrs. Devarest. I've poisoned Dr. Gelderfield's father. I've poisoned—poisoned—" The noises inside my head were getting louder. The globe that was my head was turning faster and faster. I hung on with my right hand, bracing myself against the thick cloth of the drape. There was something else I wanted to say to Lisman, but my tongue was so big and fuzzy I couldn't get it to enunciate the words. Then the drape, which was wrapped around my right hand, seemed to start pulling at my arm. It pulled until all my weight was on my right arm. I tried to scream at it, but the words wouldn't come. Then with a crash, the drape ripped loose from its fastenings, and I felt myself falling.

I was unconscious before the floor hit me.

chapter 19

I HAD THE IMPRESSION of voices hammering on my eardrums, voices that meant nothing, shouting words that were meaningless. They were yelling at me. Hands were slapping me. Boots kicked my ribs, hard police boots. Various things were happening to disturb the tranquillity of my slumbers.

After a while, these things ceased. I half awakened as someone forced my lips apart. A rubber hose gagged me as it was pushed down my throat.

I slept again.

There followed an interval when voices came and went in waves. Words which meant something fastened themselves upon my mind and then were washed out by the rolling clouds of darkness that blotted me into oblivion. But in those more lucid moments, the voices registered, and the ideas which they conveyed kept tugging at the strings of my consciousness, trying to pull me back to wakefulness.

"—pumped his stomach—hypodermic—caffeine—take effect—his confession—have to make him talk now—it will take a while."

Cold towels. The sting of a hypodermic. Hot liquid burning my throat, starting the blood circulating around my stomach. My nostrils registered the smell of coffee. A voice said, "Look, he's trying to open his eyes."

I had the impression of faces grouped around a bed, faces that were wavering and distorted as though I had been looking up at them through a stream of flowing water.

Someone seemed to be arguing. I could understand them distinctly now. "You're not going to get anywhere until some of these stimulants take effect. You may as well let him alone for the time being. I'll call you whenever he can talk coherently."

There followed a period of freedom from the annoying interruptions, then there were cold towels slapping me, and I woke up, feeling a lot better.

Bertha Cool was standing by the bedside looking at me with her glittering, angry eyes.

"Did they get there in time to save Mrs. Devarest?" I asked.

Her lips quivered with anger as she tried to speak. In the end, she had to content herself with a nod.

I waited until she could talk. "What the hell did you make that confession for?" she asked.

"So the police could get to Mrs. Devarest in time. If I'd accused someone else, they'd have come to pick me up first, and by that time it might have been too late."

I closed my eyes again, but the feeling of drowsiness was dispersing under the effects of the stimulants that had been given me. My nerves were getting that jittery, high-strung feeling that comes when I've had too many cups of coffee, and momentarily that coffee-jag feeling was gaining the ascendancy over the desire to slumber.

"How about Dr. Gelderfield's father? Did they get to him in time?"

"Yes. I could slap you for the way you've handled this."

"What's wrong with it?"

"Everything."

"What in particular?"

"You've worked us out of a job—a good job."

"I've solved the case, haven't I?"

"So what! There's no chance now of getting anything out of the insurance company. You've absolutely ruled out any chance of death by accidental means."

"No, I haven't. Dr. Devarest was murdered. Supreme Court decisions hold that a murder is a death by accidental means."

I saw the anger in her eyes give place to joyous satisfaction, and she began to purr. "Donald, you're certain?"

"Yes."

She said, "Lover, you're a card! You do the damnedest things. You wait here."

She turned and walked out of the door.

There was another period of quiet, and then a white-clad nurse stood over me. "How do you feel?" she asked.

"As though I'd been drinking about six quarts of coffee."

She held my wrist, took my pulse, nodded, picked up a glass of water, and popped a pill into my mouth.

"Take this."

After I'd swallowed the pill, she said, "Those were instructions from the police. They wanted you to be stimulated so you could talk. You won't feel any permanent ill effects, but it may be a little uncomfortable for a while."

It was all of that. I felt as though time were rushing by me, as though it were too late for everything I wanted to do or say.

"Where are the police now, if they want me so badly?"

"I don't know. The doctor went to tell them you could be interviewed. They seemed to be waiting so impatiently and—"

The door suddenly burst open, and my nerves were so jittered up I all but jumped out of bed.

Bertha Cool rushed in and said, "I guess they won't get to you for a while, Donald. Dr. Gelderfield has broken down and is making a complete confession out there in that next room. They're having your doctor as a witness, and a nurse who understands shorthand is taking it down."

"That's good. Don't bust in on me that way. I'm trembling all over. So Gelderfield is coming clean!"

"I suppose you knew it all along," said Bertha sarcastically.

"I didn't know it all along. I didn't know it soon enough. It damn near cost me my life. Don't let on to anyone though."

"Why not?"

"I don't want them to know how dumb I was. I led with my chin."

"How?"

"I told Dr. Gelderfield that Devarest must have made some call that he hadn't entered in his notebook."

"Why did you think that, Donald?"

"I knew he must have, because I felt certain he wasn't killed in his garage."

"What gave you that idea?"

I said, "Figure it out for yourself. He couldn't have gone in the garage, and then closed the door behind him. My experiment showed that the wind couldn't have closed the door. Therefore, someone must have closed the door on him. Figure out what that means, and you'll realize that Devarest was already dead when the door was closed."

"Donald dear, probably you shouldn't talk so much," Bertha said soothingly. "After all—"

"I want to talk. I feel like talking. I'm telling you there's only one way it *could* have happened. Someone drugged him, gave him a fatal dose of carbon monoxide, then took him back to his own garage, and planted the body and the evidence. I kept thinking that it must have been someone who had trapped him by asking him to make a professional call on emergency. But Devarest had the habit of marking down all of the calls he intended to make in his notebook so his bookkeeper could make the charges. I was a plain damn fool not to have thought of the right answer."

"Dr. Gelderfield?" she asked.

"Of course. Devarest was calling on Dr. Gelderfield's father, but he didn't enter that in his book because, since Dr. Gelderfield was a colleague, he was making no charge for visits to Gelderfield's father."

Bertha said, "Now, that's enough, lover. You've got to conserve your strength. After all, you had quite a dose of drug."

"And then," I said, not paying any attention to her, "I turned to Dr. Gelderfield for help and asked him if he couldn't give me some clue as to what calls Dr. Devarest might have made that wouldn't have been entered in his book— Bertha, I'm all hopped up. I'm as full of talk as a sponge is of holes. I can't *stop* talking— And *I* told him that I was going to ask Nollie Starr about it."

Bertha said, "Well?"

I said, "Don't you see? Nollie Starr would have known. If I'd asked her the question in just that way, she'd have told me that Dr. Devarest made frequent calls on Dr. Gelderfield's father, and never made any charges. Gelderfield knew I was getting pretty close to a solution of the whole business when I started asking those questions. He tried to help things along so my experiment would have been a success, and demonstrated that the east wind could have blown the garage door shut. When it turned out that, even with a reasonable amount of tampering with the door, the wind still couldn't be held accountable, Gelderfield knew that I was working on a murder theory."

"How about the gems?" Bertha asked.

"Nothing to it," I said. "Jim Timley was in love with Nollie Starr. Dr. Devarest tried to help things along. His wife found out about it, but thought it was an affair her husband was having with her secretary. She swiped the jewels herself and framed Nollie Starr."

"Then Bayley didn't have anything to do with that?"

I said, "Bayley had been planted on the job by Walter Croy. It was up to Bayley to get the safe open and get out the evidence Dr. Devarest was holding over Croy. But Mrs. Devarest mixed things up. She got Devarest to put her gems in the safe; then she sneaked them out with the aid of the combination which she'd deciphered from Dr. Devarest's notebook— Gosh, I'm wound up like an eight-day clock. I can't stop talking. Cripes, I'm jittery."

"Don't stop talking, lover. Don't stop now," Bertha said. "Keep right on. What happened then?"

I said, "You can figure it all out. After Mrs. Devarest planted the jewelry and other evidence in Nollie Starr's room, she called Dr. Devarest to come home and get the jewelry out of the safe. As soon as Devarest realized it had been taken, he knew that it was a frame-up because no one but his wife knew the jewelry was in the safe. He called Nollie Starr and told her to notify the police, and, in doing it, he managed to give her some signal that told her what she was up against."

"So that she could skip out?" Bertha asked.

"So that she could get out of the way and give Dr. Devarest a chance to go through her room and remove the evidence that had been planted. He did a pretty good job. He got the jewelry and most of the incriminating clues. He overlooked the oiled rag and a few things like that."

Bertha said, under her breath, "Pickle me for a peach."

I kept right on talking. I couldn't seem to quit. "Of course, Walter Croy thought Bayley had double-crossed him, opened the safe, and cleaned it out, but was denying he'd had anything to do with it because he wanted to keep the jewelry. So Walter then went right ahead with his case against Nadine. Mrs. Devarest had the evidence her husband was holding over Walter Croy, but she probably didn't realize its significance— My God, they must have given me all the caffeine they had in town!"

"It's all right, Donald, you've got a talking-jag. Why did Gelderfield kill him?"

"Because Gelderfield was having a little affair with Mrs. Devarest and intended to marry her. He'd been planning to murder Dr. Devarest for some time. Gelderfield's got a big house with a lot of fine furniture and virtually no servants. That tells the story. Gelderfield thought he was wealthy. Something happened to knock the props out from under him. He knew Devarest had Bright's disease, was well fixed financially, was carrying a lot of life insurance, and that Mrs. Devarest was putty in his hands."

She said, "Go on. I'm listening to every word."

"There's nothing more to talk about."

"Oh, yes, there is. Why did Dr. Devarest hire us in the first place?"

"To cover up. He told Nollie Starr to telephone the police, then tipped her off not to do it, but to skip out. When the coast was clear, Devarest went out to see Nollie Starr. He told her what had happened, promised her he'd make it all right with her, and left the jewelry with her—which was a foolish thing to do—only he'd worked out what he thought was a very fine place of concealment—cutting away the center of several books of detective stories and hiding the gems in there. The cases he'd put temporarily in the glove compartment of his automobile. After his death, Nollie Starr telephoned Jim Timley, and Timley was to get the jewels put back in the safe in some way."

"And Dr. Devarest hired us so his wife wouldn't be suspicious?"

"That's right. He didn't think there was one chance in a hundred we could find Nollie Starr, but he *did* think there was a chance we could unearth some evidence that would indicate his wife was the one who had burgled the safe. He probably intended to plant some such evidence so

214

that we'd find it."

"And Harmley?" Bertha asked.

"Harmley," I said, "just cut himself a piece of cake; and Bayley, the chauffeur, who had been playing around with Jeannette, the maid, suddenly raised his sights and went after bigger game when he thought Mrs. Devarest might be interested."

"Was she?" Bertha asked.

I grinned.

"How did Dr. Gelderfield feel about all that?" Bertha asked.

I said, "For the love of Mike, don't keep me talking. When I get started, I can't quit. Gelderfield's out there making a confession. Why don't you go out and get a load of it?"

Bertha said, "Tell me about Nadine Croy first."

I sighed, clamped my lips together, and tried to keep from talking.

"Go ahead," Bertha said. "Just that one thing, lover, and then I'll leave you alone."

I said, "Nadine was sweet on her lawyer. They'd been indiscreet. It would have raised hell with Forrest Timkan to have had his name dragged into the case with his client. So they wanted to use me as an amatory red herring. I was supposed to be the real hot-shot, sugar-daddy boy friend so far as Walter Croy was concerned. That would make Croy doubt any evidence he had pointing toward Forrest Timkan— For God's sake, Bertha, get out of here. Gelderfield may be saying something that you could use to advantage."

"How?" she asked.

"Turning it into money," I said.

That got her. She went out.

She was back in five minutes. Those five minutes seemed like ages to me. I kept my eyes shut and my lips plastered together, trying not to think and not to talk, but thoughts

215

were tumbling over in my mind like coffee grounds in a pot of coffee that has just come to a boil. I couldn't get the thought out of my mind that I'd been responsible for Nollie Starr's death. My damn fool questioning—the way I'd led with my chin—of all the damn stupidity—I wanted someone to talk to, and yet I didn't want to talk. I knew I'd go crazy if I talked, and felt that I'd burst if I didn't.

The door burst open again, and I all but jumped out of the bedclothes.

Lieutenant Lisman came in, grinning. Bertha Cool was standing just behind him. Lisman bent over the bed. "Hello, Lam. How are you feeling?"

"Like an old crate with a new super-charged motor."

He grinned. "We told them to snap you out of it fast and make you talk."

"You did too good a job."

"I've got some good news for you."

"What?"

He said, "Bertha tells me you thought it was your question that made Gelderfield kill Nollie Starr."

I nodded.

"It wasn't," Lisman said, "not directly. He's made a complete confession. He was in an awful jam. He'd been a little careless about some securities that didn't belong to him. He needed money. Mrs. Devarest was a foolish woman with a fatal heart ailment who was making advances to him. And yet such is the perversity of feminine nature"—and Lieutenant Lisman glanced obliquely at Bertha Cool—"she was jealous when she thought her own husband was playing around."

Bertha Cool said, "Nuts. That's not feminine. It's just human nature. Men are the same way—only more so."

Lisman grinned. "Gelderfield decided to get Devarest out of the way, have the widow collect the life insurance, and then marry the widow. He might have waited a while if it hadn't been that Devarest became suspicious of what was going on, and on Wednesday night, took Gelderfield to task. Gelderfield drugged his drink. Gelderfield knew all about those insurance policies and had it fixed so Devarest's death would seem to be the result of an accident, thinking that would make a difference of forty thousand bucks. Then when he realized what the policy meant by 'accidental means,' he was mad as a wet hen.

"Gelderfield knew there were two weak points in his case if anyone ever became suspicious. He felt certain Devarest had been to call on Nollie Starr that Wednesday night and probably had told her that he was going to stop by Gelderfield's on the road home."

"What was the other weak point?"

"His father. The father had heard the quarrel downstairs, but after that, he'd heard Dr. Gelderfield's automobile running for nearly an hour in Gelderfield's garage. Of course, you know what happened. Gelderfield doped a drink. When Devarest went under, he gave him a dose of carbon monoxide, then took him back to his own garage, started the car, and walked home. Like taking candy from a baby."

"What was he going to do with me?" I asked.

"He'd given you a powerful drug—left it in the bottle of Scotch, thinking that you'd be certain to take a second drink. He called up to make sure that you had."

"I know," I said. "I led with my chin."

Lisman grinned. He was really enjoying this. "You certainly did, Lam. If it hadn't been for the police, you'd have been dead by this time."

"If it hadn't been for me, you police would still be blowing your noses on your shirttails," I said.

Lisman was laughing. "Gelderfield," he said, "intended to fix things so it would look as though the chauffeur had bumped off Donald. His father's death would have been taken as a matter of course. The old man is pretty sick."

"And Nollie Starr's death?" I asked.

Lisman said, "Believe it or not, he didn't intend to pin that on Mrs. Devarest. It never occurred to him that the evidence would point to her until after you mentioned it. He'd used the string out of a surgical corset. He went to call on Nollie Starr, asked her if Dr. Devarest had mentioned anything about his plans on Wednesday night, and Nollie Starr told him she knew Devarest had gone to Gelderfield's home that night before returning to his own home, and asked Gelderfield why he hadn't said anything about it to the authorities. That signed her death warrant. Gelderfield got the potato masher out of her kitchenette under the pretext of going for a glass of water. The surgical corset string came from a corset he happened to have in his instrument bag."

"Then he didn't try to kill Mrs. Devarest when he went down there tonight?"

Lisman shook his head. "He just cleared out to give you a chance to take another doped drink and to make certain that the coast was clear so he could plant your body where the chauffeur would get the credit. He was going to marry Mrs. Devarest—as soon as he got the chauffeur out of the way, and he was going to do that by framing your murder onto him. If you damned amateurs would confide in the police once in a while instead of trying to handle it all yourself, we wouldn't have to come along and pick up the pieces and—"

I cursed him and started to climb out of bed. Lisman, the nurse, and Bertha all grabbed my shoulders and pushed me back down.

Lisman had a patronizing, self-satisfied grin. "You wouldn't want to have the doctor order a strait jacket, Lam?"

"Go to hell," I told him.

Bertha Cool put about a hundred and seventy pounds of avoirdupois across my shins. "I've got him anchored," she said. "Donald, you've got to quiet down."

Lisman kept his grin. "Nice goings, Lam. You bungled the thing all up, the way amateurs always do, but we pulled your chestnuts out of the fire for you."

"Why, damn your soul," I roared, "I—"

Bertha Cool said, "Now, Donald, you shut up. The police could still charge you on Bayley's statement."

"Nuts to them," I said.

Lisman lost his smile. "You're in the clear on everything, *if* you don't rock the boat now, Lam, so shut up. Besides, the doctor says you mustn't be disturbed. You've got to rest. You need quiet."

"Quiet!" I screamed at him. "Quiet, hell! Who do you think I am? Get off my legs, Bertha. How much caffeine did they give me, anyway?"

"It'll wear off in time," Lisman said, grinning again. "Come on, Mrs. Cool. Let's let him sleep."

Bertha said, still sitting on me, "He'll scratch your eyes out if I let him up. You better get out."

The nurse said, "Mr. Lam, the doctor's orders are that you're to stay in bed."

I said to Bertha Cool, "If you want a cut of that insurance money, get that flatfoot out of here and get that doctor to change his orders."

"Will you stay there in bed until I can do it?" Bertha asked.

Lisman realized my nerves were rubbed raw. He caught a signal from the nurse, turned, and tiptoed from the room.

"Now let your hair down," Bertha said. "He's gone. He's a good egg after all, and he knows you gave him the breaks."

The nurse said soothingly, "If you'd get out, I think I could handle him, Mrs. Cool."

Bertha looked at her hundred and twenty pounds scornfully. "You and who else?" she asked.

The nurse didn't say anything, but she exchanged some

signal with Bertha Cool, and Bertha suddenly got up off the bed and went out.

The nurse came around to sit on the edge of the bed. "Look, Mr. Lam, I know just how you feel, but I want you to listen to reason."

I started to get up.

She said, "Wait a minute. If the doctor thinks you're reacting normally, he'll let you get up and go out. Otherwise, he'll give orders to keep you in bed until you do act normally, and there are enough strait jackets here to see that you stay put. You wouldn't like that, would you?"

She smiled down at me, a schoolteacher smile, her plain, earnest face filled with sincere concern for my welfare.

I said, "I feel as though I were going to blow up. I *can't* lie still."

"You'll feel better in a few minutes. Just keep quiet now."

The door opened. Elsie Brand came in with a package under her arm. "Hello, Donald. They tell me you knocked 'em dead again."

The nurse looked Elsie over from head to foot, got up off the bed, and walked over to the other end of the room.

Elsie said, "I've seen your doctor. When I told him about the dinner you didn't eat tonight, he said maybe what you needed was food. He says you can get out of here if you're awake enough to get dressed. Donald, the butcher shops are all closed, but I know a delicatessen that sells *pretty* good steaks, and there's still some Scotch at the apartment."

I suddenly realized I was ravenous. I threw back the covers.

The nurse beckoned to Elsie Brand. I heard her say warningly in a low tone, "I wouldn't be alone with him. He's abnormally stimulated. You can't tell *what* he might do."

Elsie Brand laughed in her face.

>>> If you've enjoyed this book and would like to discover more great vintage crime and thriller titles, as well as the most exciting crime and thriller authors writing today, visit: >>>

The Murder Room
Where Criminal Minds Meet

themurderroom.com

www.ingramcontent.com/pod-product-compliance
Ingram Content Group UK Ltd.
Pitfield, Milton Keynes, MK11 3LW, UK
UKHW022315280225
455674UK00004B/317

9 781471 908842